FLAMING LONDON

by

JOE R. LANSDALE

Subterranean Press • 2005

First Edition

Trade Hardcover Edition ISBN
1-59606-025-5

Limited Edition ISBN
1-59606-026-3

Subterranean Press
PO Box 190106
Burton, MI 48519

For Bill Schafer of Subterranean Press,
and Ned the Seal, who wrote so many dime novels
and a remarkable autobiography.

Before my career as a best selling novelist, I lived an active life. I knew Captain Bemo, Doctor Momo, Buffalo Bill—still my hero—Annie Oakley—a peach of a woman—Wild Bill Hickok—a man's man...well, a seal's man as well—Sitting Bull—who invented the word stoic—I knew many others as well. I cruised beneath the seas in the Naughty Lass. I lived on the island with Doctor Momo when he made his beast men, and I am, in fact, a product of his handiwork. I even knew Tin, who came from a world far away, and I knew the Frankenstein Monster, who was one hell of a fine fella.

And I was there when the Martians came, and all the horrors that accompanied them. I was a companion of Samuel Clemens, otherwise known as the great novelist Mark Twain. I knew his friend, Jules Verne. I knew H. G. Wells. I knew the Lost Island. And I knew London when it was in flames. In my life, I have eaten many fish.

From *The Autobiography of Ned the Seal, Adventurer Extraordinaire*

Part One:

Invaders

One

A Dark Moment for Humankind

One hundred and forty million miles across the vast expanse of blackness and prickly white stars, on the planet we call Mars, the red sand shifted, and out of it rose a magnificent, blue-black, oily, machine with twenty-six enormous barrels. The barrels were cocked and loaded.

The barrels fanned wide, greased gears rotated and lifted them into their trajectories. Then there was a sound in the thin Martian air like twenty-six volcanoes erupting simultaneously. The great guns spat shiny silver cylinders dragging blue-red flame toward our Earth at a blinding speed.

From Earth the eruption was noted by astronomers, but there were no definite conclusions as to the cause. Nothing like it had ever been seen.

Twenty-six objects sped toward Earth. They were observed in our day and night skies as twenty-six flaming streaks.

They all smacked the Earth or its waters. Several in America, several in Europe, one just outside of London, one in a lake in Darkest Africa, another in India, several in the Siberian wastes, four in the Atlantic, four in the Pacific. One in the Sandwich Islands.

There were all kinds of guesses as to the source of these objects, but no one knew at the time that it was the beginning of an invasion from Mars, or that more flashes of light would follow.

And no one knew about another problem.

The very fabric of time and space was in jeopardy.

Two

Huck Bites it and Mark Twain Moves Out

In the Casbah of Tangier, Samuel Langhorne Clemens, better known as Mark Twain, sweaty as nitroglycerine, drunk as a skunk and just as smelly, resided in his stained white suit on a loose mattress that bled goose down and dust, and by lamplight he pondered the loss of his shoes and the bloated body of his pet monkey, Huck Finn.

Huck lay on the only bookshelf in the little sweat hole, and he was swollen and beaded with big blue flies. A turd about the size and shape of a fig was hanging out of his ass, and his tongue protruded from his mouth as if it were hoping to crawl away to safety. He still wore the little red hat with chin strap and the green vest Twain had put on him, but the red shorts with the ass cut out for business were missing.

Twain was uncertain what had done the old boy in, but he was dead and pantsless for whatever reason, and had managed in a final gastronomic burst, to stick that one fig-sized turd to one of the two books on the shelf, *Moby Dick*, and his distended tongue lay not far from the other book, *Twenty Thousand Leagues Under the Sea*, written by Twain's good friend Jules Verne.

Huck, bookended by sea stories, lay in dry dock.

Twain rose slowly, bent over his pet and sighed. The room stank of monkey and monkey poo. With reluctance, Twain clutched Huck by the feet, and as he lifted him, the tenacious turd took hold of the heavy tome of *Moby Dick* and lifted it as well. Twain shook Huck, and *Moby Dick*, along with the turd, came loose. Twain then peeked carefully out the only window at the darkness of the Casbah below, and tossed Huck through the opening.

It was a good toss and Huck sailed.

Twain heard a kind of whapping sound, realized he had tossed Huck with such enthusiasm, he had smacked the wall on the other side of the narrow alley.

It was a cold way to end a good friendship, but Twain hardly felt up to burying the little bastard, and was actually pissed that the beast had died on him. Huck had wandered off for a day, come back sickly, vomited a few times, then set about as if to doze on the bookshelf.

Sometime during the night, Twain heard a sound that he thought was the release of his own gas, but upon lighting the lamp, found it in fact to be Huck, who had launched that sticky, fig-shaped turd. He saw the little monkey kick a few times and go still.

Twain, too drunk to do anything, too drunk to care, put out the lamp and went back to sleep.

A few hours later, hung over, but sober enough to wonder if it had all been a dream, lit his lamp to find that Huck was indeed dead as the Victorian novel, but without the shelf life. Flies were enjoying themselves by surveying every inch of Huck, and due to the intense African heat, Huck had acquired an aroma that would have swooned a vulture.

No question about it. He had to go.

With Huck dead and tossed, Twain decided to pour himself a drink, but discovered he had none. The goatskin of wine was empty. Twain dropped it on the stone floor, stood on it, hoping to coax a few drops to the nozzle, but, alas, nothing. Dry as a Moroccan ditch in mid-summer.

Twain removed his coat, shook it out, draped it over the back of the chair, seated himself. He sat there and thought about what to do next. He had sold all of his book collection, except *Twenty Thousand Leagues,* which was signed, and the be-turded *Moby Dick*. He didn't even have copies of his own books.

It was depressing.

When he was strong enough, he rose and made coffee in his little glass pot. It was weak coffee because there were only yesterday's grounds left, and the biscuit tin contained only a couple of stale biscuits which he managed to eat by dipping them in the coffee.

By the time he had finished breakfast, light was oozing through the window and he could hear the sounds of the Casbah below.

Blowing out his lamp, he recovered *Moby Dick* from the floor, wiped it clean with a cloth and the remains of the coffee. It left a slight stain, coffee, not shit, but he hoped it wouldn't damage what value the book might have. Tangier was full of readers of most anything in English (except his books, it seemed) and he might get a few coins for it, as well as for the signed copy of *Twenty Thousand Leagues*.

It would be just enough money for a real meal of fruit and olives, and a bit of wine, as well as the rent. Which seemed pointless.

What after that? There was no place for him to work, and his new novel was going about as well as his life had. Everyone he knew and loved was dead. Well, almost. There were a few friends, Verne among them.

Twain searched about and found his missing shoes, then he grabbed a big white canvas bag and stuffed it with a few belongings, his manuscript in progress, gathered up the two books and headed out into the Casbah. As he climbed down the narrow stairs and rushed into the street, he came upon Huck's body being feasted upon by dogs.

The biggest of the dogs, a mongrel with one eye and scum around it, wrestled Huck away from the others, and darted down the street with his prize, the monkey's tail dragging on the flagstones.

Twain sighed.

Perhaps when he died, that was what was to become of him. Tossed in the street, eaten by dogs.

It was better than being savaged to death by book critics. The sonsabitches.

The street stank of yesterday's fish and today's fresh fish. Blood dripped from the tables and gathered in little rust-colored pools and slipped in between the grooves in the stones. The reek of ripe olives bit the air and chewed at Twain's nostrils. He wandered the crooked streets, which just six months ago he would have found harder to navigate than the Minotaur's maze, and came upon Abdul laying out his sales goods on a worn but still beautiful Moroccan rug of blue, green, and violet. Among the items on the rug were a few books. Twain recognized titles he had written, books from his very own collection. Each one of them reminded him of the few coins he had contributed to drink and women, mostly drink.

Abdul eyed Twain with his bag and two books under his arm.

"My friend. More books. You can see I do not need them."

"These are my last books, Abdul. I sell these, I'm taking the ferry to Spain."

"And what there? You should stay here among friends."

"You old pirate. You've given me little for what I've sold you. These are fine books."

"They are not worth much."

"I sold you copies of my own novels, signed."

"Alas, they are not worth much either. Perhaps had they not been signed."

"Very funny, Abdul. If I didn't feel like an elephant had sat on my head, I would give you a good old-fashioned American ass whipping."

Abdul pulled back his robe and revealed in his belt a curved, holstered blade with an ornate handle of jewels and silver.

"Well, maybe I wouldn't," Twain said. "Will you buy the books, Abdul?"

"Promise you have no more?"

"I promise."

Twain squatted, laid them on the blanket Abdul had stretched out on the ground.

"What's this stain on *Moby Dick?*"

"A fig got squashed on it. My monkey did it."

"Where is Huck?"

"He leaped out of the window this morning and committed suicide. Landed right on his head."

Abdul looked at him.

"Even monkeys fall out of trees," Twain said.

"Very well, I will give you..."

"In dollars, Abdul."

"Very well, I will give you four dollars."

"Jesus Christ, the *Twenty Thousand Leagues* is signed to me by Jules Verne. The both of us certainly have some coinage for collectors."

"Okay. How about I give you ten dollars?"

"How about you give me fifteen?"

"Deal."

Three

A Ferry Ride, an Injured Seal

It was more money than Twain expected to receive for the books, so he bought some figs, a skin of water, and boarded the ferry to Spain. It took most of the day, and the sea was choppy. Twain lost his figs and water early on, throwing them up in a brown stream over the side.

As he leaned over the railing, watched the water churn below, he considered losing himself as well, but gradually came to his senses. He realized that he was feeling better as the wine wore off, realized too this was the first time in six months he had been truly sober.

It wasn't a great feeling, but it really wasn't that bad either.

Upon arriving on the coast of Spain, he and the passengers, as well as a dozen goats and a cage of chickens, disembarked. It felt good to be on solid ground, and after buying some coffee in a little outdoor cafe, fending off a half dozen souvenir peddlers and a fat Spanish whore who wanted to sell him a quickie, or for half the price, squeeze him off between her legs, he decided to splurge another coin and catch a cart ride to where Verne was staying, working on yet another successful novel.

Twain envied Verne. He seemed able to write at any time and under any circumstance. As of late, all he could think about was the death of his wife, Olivia, and the death of his daughters. Susy by disease, Jean, drowned in a tub while having a fit, and Clara, married and gone from him, living somewhere in Europe, a place unbeknownst to him since beginning his wanderings. He hoped her life was good. He hoped he would find her again someday. He hoped even more that some of his old self would return to him, like a lost dog, worn out and tired, looking for a familiar bed, a currycomb, a pat on the head, and a good meal.

As the cart clattered along, Twain noted the beautiful coast. Perhaps this was the key to Verne's success. A beautiful view. The Casbah was interesting and exciting in its own way, but it wasn't beautiful, and too much excitement and noise did not a good writer make. Here you had the ocean and the shoreline with natural white sand, and there were the rocks upon which the ocean foamed, and way out beyond that fine blue water, a thin brown strip that was Africa, the coast of Morocco from which he had come.

As they neared Verne's residence, Twain stopped the driver, paid him, and in spite of his old aching bones, decided to walk along the coast and wind his way to where Verne lived in a beautiful villa on a rise of white rocks overlooking the sea.

As he walked along the beach, his bag slung over his shoulder, Twain discovered a strange thing. A large black shape with something shiny attached to it lay near the ocean on the sand. At first he couldn't place what it was. It appeared to be an oilskin bag with something metal hanging out of one end, but upon closer examination he was amazed to discover it was a seal. A seal with a metal object, a box, fastened to its head. There were a number of deep red cuts in the seal's body, and a chunk had been taken out of one flipper by what were obviously some very nasty teeth.

Shark teeth, Twain figured.

Twain bent over the seal, nudged it with his foot. The seal opened one eye.

Very slowly the seal rolled over. Twain saw there was a cord around his neck, and fastened to that was a writing tablet without paper, and a stubby pencil. There was also a chain around the seal's neck, and from that hung a pair of sand-sprinkled spectacles.

He discovered there was another thing even more amazing than a seal with a metal cap, pad and pencil, and reading glasses about its neck.

There were little thumbs growing from its flippers.

Four

The Great Jules Verne, Ned's Story, a Shape beneath the Canvas

When Twain arrived at Verne's villa pulling the seal on his formerly white coat, Verne was on the second floor landing, sitting with pen and paper, working on a dark novel about Paris, thinking about how old he felt, the loss of his wife and children, who had gone off to live somewhere in France with the explorer Phileas Fogg.

The dirty bastard.

Verne tried to concentrate on his work.

He had submitted pages of his novel to his editor, but the editor had been appalled. Much too noir for them, lacked the glitter of his other novels, and they felt his readers would be disappointed.

It certainly was a dark book, and not optimistic in the least, but the thing was, Verne wasn't feeling too optimistic right then, and the novel reflected that. He felt he had fallen into a trap of writing only what many were now calling children's adventure stories. He longed to reach deeper and write darker. He wished he had his children back, and his wife had a hot croissant up her ass, and Fogg had one too. Neither croissant buttered, and both day old and stiff.

He did have his experiments, his plans for devices that he worked on from time to time, and they had of course made some impact on the world, but so far their use and knowledge of them were restricted primarily to himself and his servant, Passepartout, and to a handful of rich associates; the devices were far too expensive to give away, and patents had to be protected.

He was thinking about these things as he pondered his maligned manuscript with distracted concentration, so when he saw his old friend Samuel, Mark Twain to the world, he was surprised and heartened to have a break from his work and editorial troubles, as well as curious to discover what his bedraggled friend was pulling on top of his coat.

Downstairs, Verne met Twain in the front yard and saw what he had. When Verne spoke English, his French accent was noticeable, but not too heavy. He had been practicing his English for some time, and had learned much about American colloquialism from the works of Twain, though he still had the occasional French phrasing. When he spoke to his friend, he called him by his real name, Samuel.

When Twain saw Verne, he smiled. "Jules."

"My friend, Samuel. You have a seal on your coat."

"Yes, I do."

"He is dead, monsieur?"

"No, he's not. He's been bitten by sharks, but he's alive. See that metal hat. It's bolted to his head. Fixed that way. Look at that stuff around his neck. What do you make of it?"

"I make nothing of it. Shall we put him in the barn?"

———◦•◦———

In the barn, Verne used a hand pump and water hose to wash down the seal, then examined his wounds. "We'll need someone who can sew good stitches. I'll make a call."

When Verne left, Twain made the seal as comfortable as possible, saw a large canvas draped over a large form. At the bottom of the canvas, he could see something shiny. He wondered what was beneath the canvas, and under ordinary circumstance, might have taken a look, but he didn't wish to leave the injured seal, and besides, his age had caught up with him a bit. Now that he had gotten comfortable, sitting on the ground, he didn't want to get up unless it was absolutely necessary.

———◦•◦———

Verne went to the house, cranked the phone and spoke in Spanish. When he came back to the barn, Twain was holding the seal's head up, giving him a drink from a water dipper.

"That is strange," said Vern. "He takes that like a man."

The seal raised its flipper, and working its thumb against the skin of the appendage, made a snapping sound.

"Well, I will be, how is it you Americans say? I be damn."

"Close enough."

The seal tapped the pad on its chest, took hold of the pen.

"My God," Twain said. "He wants writing paper."

"That is not possible."

The seal snapped both thumbs against his flippers and made a kind of whistling sound with his mouth, then slapped both flippers against the pad and took hold of the pencil with one thumb and flipper and made a writing motion.

"Now I've seen it all," Verne said.

"Not if he actually writes something, you haven't."

⇒•⇐

Verne ran to the house, procured paper and a better pencil. When he returned with the writing materials, the seal sat up on its hind end, folding its flipper-tipped tail beneath it, cocked its back against the water pump, placed the glasses on its nose, took the writing supplies and wrote in big block letters.

MY NAME IS NED. I WAS THE BOON COMPANION OF BUFFALO BILL CODY, WHO WAS EATEN BY SHARKS. I WAS INJURED BY SHARKS. I LIKE SLOW SWIMS AND BIG LIVE FISH AND SOMETIMES A BEACH BALL TO BALANCE ON MY NOSE, THOUGH I KNOW IT'S IMMATURE.

I DO NOT LIKE SHARKS.

I DO LIKE FISH. DID I MENTION THAT?

"Holy shit," Twain said. "A goddamn note-writing seal."

The seal continued to write, passing along pages as he filled them in his large block printing.

HERE IS MY STORY. I WAS MADE BY A MAN NAMED DOCTOR MOMO. HE LIVED ON AN ISLAND. I SPENT MUCH OF MY TIME WITH CAPTAIN BEMO ON THE *NAUGHTY LASS*. ONCE I WAS A REGULAR SEAL. NOW I AM SPECIAL.

"Holy Mother of God, give Jesus the apple," Verne said. "I wrote a novel based on this very interesting man, Captain Bemo. Not all true, a novel mind you, with name changes, but with much biographical detail. This is amazing. This seal claims to have known the real Captain Bemo, on which my Nemo is based. I have also heard of this Momo. A scientist. About half crazy was the rumor. H. G. Wells has written a story about him. He calls him Moreau."

"Let him write, Jules," Twain said.

I HELPED BEMO AND MOMO DO RESEARCH. I WAS ABLE TO DO THIS BECAUSE DOCTOR MOMO ENHANCED MY ALREADY CONSID-ERABLE INTELLIGENCE WITH THIS DEVICE YOU SEE ON MY HEAD. HE DID THINGS TO MY BRAIN. AMPLIFIED IT. THE DEVICE COVERS MY BRAIN, PROTECTS IT. MOMO BECAME STRANGE. HE GRAFTED A HORSE PENIS ONTO HIMSELF. HE MADE PEOPLE OUT OF ANIMALS AND PIECES OF FLESH. BUFFALO BILL, WILD BILL HICKOK, ANNIE OAKLEY AND SITTING BULL ALL CAME TO MOMO'S ISLAND, HAV-ING CRASHED IN THE SEA. BUFFALO BILL WAS ONLY A HEAD. IT WAS IN A JAR POWERED BY BATTERIES AND SOME KIND OF LIQUID. THEY HAD THE FRANKENSTEIN MONSTER WITH THEM. THERE WAS A TIN MAN WHO WORKED FOR DOCTOR MOMO. HE AND THE MON-STER FELL IN LOVE. I THINK THEY MAY HAVE DROWNED ON THE *NAUGHTY LASS,* AS DID WILD BILL HICKOK AND ANNIE OAKLEY, AND I SUPPOSE SITTING BULL AND A WOMAN MOMO MADE NAMED CAT. BUFFALO BILL'S HEAD WAS EATEN BY SHARKS. I WAS BITTEN BY SHARKS. I SURE COULD USE SOME FISH.

"What happened to Momo and Bemo?" Verne asked.

Ned shook his head, wrote: I DO NOT KNOW. I THINK THEY ARE DEAD. MOMO'S BOAT RAMMED THE *NAUGHTY LASS* AND SUNK IT, I THINK. HE WAS PROBABLY ON BOARD. THE ONLY WAY HE COULD HAVE LIVED IS IF HE COULD LIVE IN PIECES, LIKE A PUZZLE. DO YOU LIKE THE DIME NOVELS ABOUT BUFFALO BILL CODY? DO YOU HAVE ANY FISH?

"I don't have any fish," Twain said, "but I do like the novels about Buffalo Bill. Can't say they are well written, but they are entertaining. Ned, I am Samuel Clemens, though I go by the name Mark Twain as well, which is the name I write under. This is Jules Verne."

Ned stiffened. His whiskers wiggled. He slapped his flippers together. He snatched up the pencil, wrote:

AFTER THE ADVENTURES OF BUFFALO BILL AND THE DIME NOVELS, I LIKE YOU TWO BEST. ABOUT THE SAME, ACTUALLY. I HAVE READ *HUCK FINN* AND *TOM SAWYER,* AND I HAVE READ *JOURNEY TO THE CENTER OF THE EARTH, FROM THE EARTH TO THE MOON,* AND IF YOU WILL FORGIVE ME, I TRIED TO READ YOUR STORY ABOUT BEMO. HE WAS NOTHING LIKE THAT. HE WAS QUITE SHY, ACTUALLY. HE DID DO MUCH THAT YOU WROTE ABOUT, BUT NOT ALL OF IT. MIND YOU, I WASN'T THERE DURING ALL THOSE EVENTS, BUT I DID HAVE THE LUXURY OF KNOWING THE MAN.

HE HAD GAS PROBLEMS. THAT'S ANOTHER FACT NOT WELL KNOWN. YOU MIGHT WANT TO WRITE THAT DOWN IN CASE YOU DO A REVISED VERSION OF YOUR BOOK. SEALS DON'T REALLY MIND THAT, HOWEVER. REMEMBER. WE EAT RAW FISH. AND, OF COURSE, FISH EAT US. SHARKS TRIED TO EAT ME. I TRIED TO SAVE THE HEAD OF BUFFALO BILL...DID I SAY I DO NOT LIKE SHARKS AND THAT I WOULD LIKE SOME FISH?

"Yes," Verne said, "you did. And I read something about Buffalo Bill being a living head powered by batteries. Some kind of accident. Saved by a scientist, some such thing...And I remember reading in the papers about part of the Wild West Show being lost over the Pacific ocean. I think this little seal is telling the truth, Samuel."

Ned slapped a flipper on the ground. Hard.

He wrote: OF COURSE I AM. DO I LOOK LIKE A LIAR TO YOU?

⸺◈⸺

The man Verne had called arrived and stitched up Ned to the sound of grunts and squeals while Verne and Twain held the poor seal. Once, Ned was able to snatch up the pencil and paper Verne had provided. He wrote: WHERE'S THE ANESTHESIA? WANT IT. GOT TO HAVE IT. WANT IT BAD. TELL THIS HORRIBLE MAN TO GET OFF OF ME AND TAKE HIS NEEDLES WITH HIM. OH, YOU ASSHOLES.

Twain wrestled the pencil and paper away from Ned, said, "Sorry, Ned. For your own good."

"My God," the veterinarian said in French. "He writes."

"Yes he does," Twain said, being able to understand French well enough. "And neatly."

"How is that possible?" asked the vet.

"It's a trick." Twain said.

"With mirrors and such?" the veterinarian asked.

Twain looked at Vern. They both looked at the vet.

Verne said, "Of course. Mirrors."

Five

A Meal, Pleasant Conversation, a Duck Toy

That evening they dined in Verne's fine dining room, waited on by a servant dressed in crisp black pants, white jacket and black bow tie. Verne was now dressed in smoking jacket and loose pants and Moroccan slippers. He had provided a similar outfit for Twain.

Earlier, while removing these items from his closet, he had stumbled over a red fez with a golden tassel that had been given him by a friend. He had never worn it. Ned saw this while waiting for Verne to supply fresh clothes for Twain. It was obvious to Verne that he was taken with it, so he gave it to the little seal, fastened it over the metal box on Ned's head. Ned looked rather suave in the fez, like a seal of great importance and wealth with a harem.

With his stitches in place, Ned forgave them for holding him down. The pain had passed. And besides, he had a neat as hell red hat.

Ned was placed in a portable Victorian-style tub with fresh water. Next to it was a long low table on which sat bowls of fresh sardines, fish oil, and wine. And, of course, a napkin. Floating on the water was a rubber duck toy. At first, Ned resented it, but discovered it squeaked when he squeezed it, and he eventually found it comforting. He balanced it on his nose and made seal sounds.

The servant, Passepartout, who had been with Verne for years, appeared to be totally unperturbed by an injured seal near the dining table in a tub with a rubber duck. He looked as if he had seen it all, and then some. He poured the seal's wine with the same panache he poured all wine.

Upon completion of pouring, Ned took his pencil and pad from the little table and wrote: THANK YOU, KIND SIR.

In French, Passepartout told Ned he was quite welcome. Then, said the same in English.

Verne thanked Passepartout, and the servant went away, saying, "Very good, monsieur."

"When we finish," Verne said, "we will retire to the study for cigars."

Ned took up his pad, wrote, and held up what he had written:

NO THANK YOU. SMOKING IS BAD FOR YOU.

"Very well," Verne said. "Then, for you, smoked herring. Will that be sufficient?"

Ned wrote again, held up his pad on which he had written:

SMOKED HERRING IS NOT BAD FOR YOU. HOW MUCH SMOKED HERRING?

"A lot," Verne said. "And tomorrow, I have another present for you. Something I designed some time ago."

Ned, in anticipation of the herring, ate his sardines and drank his wine, dozed in his tub, dreamed of female seals with long eyelashes. From time to time the sound of the duck being squeaked could be heard.

Six

Cylinders from Space, a Hole in the Ground, a Strange Ray

While the three companions were enjoying dinner on the beautiful coast of Spain, on the outskirts of foggy London the first of the bullets, or cylinders as some described them, screwed open with a hiss of steam and a red and yellow wink of light.

The screwing motion caused the lid to fall off, smack in the dust. A crowd, which had gathered at the rim of the crater caused by the impact of the cylinder, watched carefully. They had been watching for nearly a half hour.

"It's opening," said a short stocky man in the back of the crowd.

This was, of course, obvious. The short stocky man had been giving them a play by play since the crowd first arrived. As there was little to see other than the cylinder, he took it upon himself to describe the steam coming from the interior of the device, and was quick to describe it in excruciating detail, as if everyone present was blind.

"See the steam coming out. More steam than before. A lot of steam's coming out," he said.

This was true.

"Now the lid has fallen off. See that?"

Everyone saw that.

"Now there's some light. Do you see the light?"

The light was pretty obvious. Red and yellow.

"There's something moving in there. Did you see the shadow?"

Suddenly, without warning, a little man in the crowd screamed something impossible to understand, leaped on the explainer and began beating him. "We see it. We see it, you dumb bastard."

Police arrived and promptly jerked the small man off of the explainer, hauled him away, stuck him in the back of a police wagon. The police returned to the scene.

"Thank you, officers," said the explainer. "He had gone mad, he had. Oh, look, look, the shadow is growing larger."

Indeed, it had grown, and something was starting to come out of the cylinder.

"It's a bloomin' octopus," said the explainer.

In fact, a tentacle, reminiscent of an octopus, was waving out of the opening, as if hoping to snag something floating in the air.

"They've got a bloomin' octopus in that tube," said the explainer. "Can you see that? A bloomin' octopus. Now he's comin' out. More of him. You see that?"

The police officers looked at one another.

"Ah, two tentacles."

The higher ranking officer turned to the other. "Go let the little man out of the cage, will you?"

"Certainly."

"It's crawling out," said the explainer.

"Excuse me, sir," said the officer. "That is quite clear to all of us. Would you please shut your bleeding mouth."

"Why, I can't believe that. Did you hear that, friends. The officer told me to shut my bleedin'—"

It was just one quick shot of the billy club, between the eyes, and down went the explainer. The little man who had been caged came back with the lower ranked officer, stood with them, glanced down at the unconscious explainer.

"Should he awake," said the officer, "one word from him, you have our permission to finish what you started."

A shriek went up from the crowd.

A bulbous head with two red eyes peeked out of the mouth of the cylinder. Its two arms, which continued to wave, were joined by two others. It did very much look like an octopus.

It glanced up at the crowd with its odd red eyes, quivered its beak-like lips, omitted a sound like someone trying to breathe after running a fast mile, then retreated into the cylinder.

"It's frightened," said the little man who had jumped the explainer.

"You're not going to start now, are you?" said one of the officers.

Inside the cylinder, there was a sound like something being snapped together. Then there was a guttural sound like someone displeased. This was followed by more snapping and more guttural noises, as if some sort of trouble was being had with the fastening of a device.

⋙⋘

Martian Translation of Gutteral Noise:

"It goes in the other hole, Gooldaboo."

"Which hole?"

"That hole."

"I don't get it. This hole?"

"No. One of your assholes. For heaven's sakes, give me that. Damn. That got me in the eye. You are always dooddiddledooin something. That could have put my eye out. There...I'll take care of this. You just sit there. And don't touch anything, Gooldaboo."

"Yes sir/ma'am."

———

As the people watched, metal tubing poked out of the cylinder, followed by what looked like an octopus with rectal pain. It scooted along the rough ground making a number of faces with its flexible skin and long broad mouth, which was quite unlike an octopus. It set the little framework of tubing on the edge of the cylinder, rotated it.

The other creature appeared, carrying a long thin tube of light. This was placed in one end of the cylinder. The octopus reached a tentacle around the end of the tubing and pulled. It extended. He rotated the cylinder again, pointing the tip of it at the crowd.

"What do you think he's doin'?" asked someone.

"Could that be a gun?" someone else said.

"Shit," said one of the policeman.

And then there came a guttural sound from one of the creatures—

—good-bye funny things—

—and the tube spat out a rod of light. The light hit the crowd. The crowd glowed. The crowd disappeared. Left in its place were piles of black dust.

The creatures flapped their tentacles wildly, made sounds that even humans would have recognized as laughing. One of the Martians climbed up on the edge of the crater, turned both assholes to where the crowd had been and cut an excruiating fart that flapped the edges of both his anuses, turned and said:

Take that, you inferior fuckers.

Seven

A Meteor, a Tidal Wave,
the Martian Machines

Meanwhile, back at the villa...

Vern, Twain, and Ned had gathered in the study. Ned was enjoying pickled herring while his rescuers smoked large cigars amongst thousands of volumes of books. One side of the room, the only side without books, was made up of numerous glass windows, and there was a fine view of the moonlit ocean. The waves came in white and silver whirls and burst against the white rocks on the shore and sent up spray that, in the moonlight, looked like an explosion of pearls.

"Look," said Twain.

The night sky, as if clawed, was bleeding a horde of red marks.

"Meteors, I presume," said Verne.

"Yes," said Twain. "Most beautiful."

"Look at that," said Verne, "they do not seem to be burning up in the atmosphere. Why, look there."

One of the red scars stripped across the sky and grew in size until it was a ball of red.

"My god," Verne said. "It's going to make landfall."

"More like wet fall," Twain said.

The great ball of fire struck the ocean with a hard blast of white steam. The ocean waters rolled up high and dropped down and came upon the shore with a rush that caused the waves to rise as high as Verne's house on the hill, all the way up to the glass windows of the study. It struck them with such force the glass collapsed, the water washed in, overturning furniture, knocking books from the cases, lifting Twain and Verne and Ned up and down, and then the water washed out again, fast as it had come in, took the three with it, but crashed them against a wall, left them lying on the floor amongst wetness, seaweed, fish, and the wet pulpy pages of books.

Ned darted for the fish, finding one large creature to his taste. He tore into it instantly.

"Damn," said Vern. "Now that was unusual."

"What I'm wondering," said Twain, "is what happened to all the others."

"Others?"

"The meteors," Twain said.

"What I'm wondering is how much of my home has been ruined."

Next morning, Verne called in workers to clean up his library, replace the glass. During the day, he, Ned and Twain took the dampened books—only a handful had been ruined—out into the sunlight, opening them to dry on the rocks beneath the warm Spanish sun.

Twain had been given a new set of clothes by Verne, a nice white suit and shirt with white socks and black shoes.

Verne had provided this because he did not like to wear white as much as Twain. He was dressed as usual in a black suit and white dress shirt. He had even bothered to tie a loose, thick, black tie about his neck in a bow.

Ned had received the present Verne had promised. A device Verne called The Cruiser. A floating device, powered by air and by a core of uranium. The device had a fold-down step, and this led through a flap-open gate, a wraparound body. It was large enough for Ned and two others, if the three were willing to be pressed together tight.

Inside the open air machine, standing slightly higher than the encircling railing, was a control box on a post. There were but a few switches. It was essentially a disk with a railing and a gear box on a support.

"It runs about six inches to twelve inches over the ground. A friend of mine in London invented the fuel core. He thinks that it will allow him to travel through time, this fuel. I think he is an idiot in that respect, but in all others he is a genius. The device is designed to create a current of air beneath, and this current will carry you over either land or water. One thing that is most unique, is that by pulling the red lever the sides will collapse and the surface on which you stand will also collapse, forming a kind of disk. The disk is very light, and can be reinstated by gripping the sides with your hands, or thumbs in your case, Ned, and pulling. You must watch though, for it will spring to life and knock you on your ass. Place it on the ground, so that when it springs, it will spring up, and you will be standing to the side. But it is ready now. Climb in."

With Verne at his side, Ned learned to work the device, and with the tassel on his fez popping in the wind, Ned rode about over the shoreline and even over the water, cruising at a fairly good clip.

Ned was so excited he squealed. Verne had also provided him with a new pad. It was not made of paper, but was more like a white board. The pencil, which hung by a strong cord from the pad, was one with which you could write on the board, and erase with a wipe of your hand. Strangely, it left no stains on flesh or seal skin.

"This way," Verne said, "you need not worry about paper, or for that matter, the whole thing becoming damp. You can swim with it around your neck. There's a light vest that goes with it, and you can push the pad against the vest, and it will stick. I call this, well, I call this sticky. Water will not loosen it, but with a quick flip of flipper and thumb you can remove it and write on it. There is also a cord attached around your neck for added insurance."

After an hour or so of experimenting with the near silent craft, Verne was confident Ned had it. They coasted back to shore where Twain waited.

"What a device, Jules," Twain said. "You are truly a genius. Like me."

Jules grinned.

"Passepartout is as much genius as I. Or as you. He actually put it together. I provided the blueprint, the idea. And my friend in London—"

"Would that be Wells?"

"It would, provided, as I have said, the fuel. Shall we continue our work?"

—=◦·◦=—

It was midday, and the books were drying well. Because of this, and his time spent with the delighted seal, Twain noted that Jules' depression, due to the destruction of part of his house and books, was passing. He was glad. Jules was a good man. A little more successful than himself…Well, a lot. But a good man. He just wished he were the one who was successful and Jules had a corn cob up his ass.

Or sometimes he wished that.

He felt bad about wishing that, but, alas, there it was.

He had liked being rich and famous, and now he was only famous, and he realized now that rich was probably better. And, frankly, he wasn't sure how famous he was anymore.

He missed America. He missed his home. He missed his dead wife and daughters. Wondered where in Europe his other daughter resided. They had, due to him and his adventures with John Barleycorn, lost contact.

While Twain was reflecting on this, as well as examining a copy of *Don Quixote* he heard a noise, lifted his head, spotted something rising from the sea. It was a machine. It had long, flexible, metallic legs and a body like a grand daddy long-legged spider. It stood high up on its shiny silver legs and it moved quickly, as if its feet were on a hot griddle. The torso, if it could be called that, was fronted by a window of glass (1), and behind the glass were two strange creatures flailing with octopus arms at numerous controls. They almost seemed to be struggling with the gears and levers.

A little rod rotated under the torso of the machine, and out of it burst a ray of light that hit the rocks between where Verne and Twain stood, disintegrating them. The explosion knocked Verne and Twain winding. Ned was able to avoid the brunt of the blast, but he too was knocked by the shock waves.

"Jumping horn toads," Twain said, as he pushed himself to his feet. "Shit, Jules. It's still coming."

And it was. It was on land now, and the two creatures behind the glass were definitely struggling at the controls. The way their tentacles whipped about, they looked like confetti in a windstorm.

---

1. It appeared to be glass to Twain, Verne and Ned, but actually it was a kind of Martian plastic, very hard, and waterproof.

Interior of the Martian War Machine, and we've got:
mine! ultu gets to kill.
no. mine. ultu can suck my asses.
fatty.
smelly.

Twain and Verne could not have known that the aliens, though wise and developed in the ways of machinery and invention, were, as far as emotions, as immature as six-year-olds. Even as Ned, Twain and Verne climbed into the device Verne called an Air Cruiser and made their exit, inside the war machine a fight broke out.

---

mine!
no. mine!
remove your tentacles, you assholes.
you. you assholes.
i got your assholes, you bilbo sucking—

Gears were touched that shouldn't have been touched. The legs of the stalking device twisted and wadded up and down went the device, striking the glass, shattering it, rolling over and over, and finally, with the glass now pointing toward the sky, one of the creatures pushed at the shattered pieces and finally worked them free and scuttled out of the machine, bleeding green ichor.

mine, said the creature.

To the ears of humans, these words would have sounded like coughs and sneezes.

all mine.

The creature crawled over the rocks, and one of its tentacles, which had been cut badly in the crash, came loose and stayed behind.

orifice excrement, it said. that is not some good at all.

Inside the machine, the other creature did not move. One of its eyes had come loose of its tendons, cut on a fragment of smashed metal, and it rolled out on the rocks and lay there like a giant medicine ball with an iris painted on it.

The crawling creature soon ceased to crawl and lay on the beach. Quite still, and quite dead, looking for solace, poked one of its own tentacles up its ass.

—◦—

Looking back, observing this, our formerly escaping trio shot the cruiser back to where the creature lay sprawled on the sand like a beached squid.

"What in hell?" Twain said, climbing down from the machine, poking at the beast with the toe of his shoe.

Verne followed. The fez festooned seal kept his place at the controls, nervously checking out the sea and the surrounding landscape for more attackers. He also wondered if the creatures were edible. They looked like things he had eaten. Only what he had eaten had been smaller. But they looked very similar.

"The meteors," Verne said. "They contained these life forms. It's the only possibility. My guess is, due to recent articles I've read about canals on Mars, and the relative closeness of Mars to Earth, these, my good friend, are, in fact, invaders from that world."

"No shit?"

"No shit. I wonder what happened here? How they crashed?"

"A malfunction of some kind. Whatever, it was good for us."

Ned made a whistling noise, slapped his flippers together, pointed toward the sea with one of them.

Out there, rising out of the water, were more of the machines.

"Damn be it all and such," Verne said, trying to sound American but failing miserably. "We must warn Passepartout. Would you do that, Samuel? I will prepare our escape. I know just the thing. Meet me in the barn."

Twain raced off for the house, while Verne and Ned headed toward the barn in the cruiser.

Eight

Passepartout's Blueprint, Pursuit at Sea, Mooned by Aliens

In the barn, Verne leaped from the cruiser, proceeded to the tarp and using a pocket knife cut the ropes and removed it.

Beneath lay a shiny craft. It was long with a point on one end and glass slanted into a windshield. It had one great fin that started on the roof and ran to the tail.

Twain and Passepartout came racing through the open barn door. Twain said, "If you've got a plan, might I suggest you put it to use. Those things are everywhere now, out of the sea, making kindling out of your house."

"I have this machine, my friend."

"Please tell me it does more than open cans."

Verne produced a key from his pocket, stuck it in the side of the machine. There was a hissing sound, like the air coming out of a bicycle tire, and a trap door came open slowly, guided by hydraulics and a puff of steam.

"Climb in," Verne said.

Ned rode the cruiser inside and managed by himself to collapse it. He nosed it up and rolled it behind a curved couch at the rear of the craft.

Once they were all inside, Verne closed the door, set about spinning a wheel that battened down the door firmly.

"Watertight," Verne said. "Powered by Mr. Wells' invention. As well as steam."

Verne hustled to the front of the craft. The same key that opened the door fit into a slot on the instrument panel. Verne turned it, the machine hissed, the panel lit up like the U.S. on the Fourth of July.

"That's pretty fine," Twain said. "But does it do anything besides look pretty?"

Passepartout said, "Might I suggest we strap ourselves in the seats. Tight."

Passepartout hastened to do just that, but not before he strapped Ned into his seat. Ned's seat was behind Verne's, Passepartout was behind the seat that Twain took, which was to the right of Verne.

"How do you say it," Verne said, "grab you ankles and kiss your asshole, because here we go? Or, I hope. This is its maiden voyage."

"What?" Twain said.

"First time, monsieur."

"But where do we go, Jules? The barn door is over there, to the right."

There was a big lever on Verne's left. He popped it free, jerked a small gear forward, put his foot on something, and the sleek machine rose up on a set of rubber-wrapped wheels (one front, one rear), pooted a burst of fire and steam out of its ass, and leaped.

It seemed as if suddenly the barn wall jumped at them.

Twain threw his hands over his eyes.

The craft hit the wall with a sound like grapeshot, then they were through it amidst a crack and a rain of splinters.

The craft hit the shoreline in an instant, dove into the sea, raced across it like a shark, water spraying the windshield like bulldog drool.

"My God, a submersible," Twain said. "Like in your book. *Twenty Thousand Leagues.*"

"No, it does not go under," Verne said. "Not completely. It is a very fast boat. In fact, I call it a speedy boat. And it can serve as a land vehicle. And, like a flying fish, it can fly, or rather leap, short distances."

"Damn, that was some takeoff," Twain said. "I think I'm sitting a foot higher in my seat, if you know what I mean."

"If you feel the need," Verne said, "There is a toilet in the back. The feces are absorbed by chemicals, flushed out the rear of the boat. I believe once the chemicals do their work it is harmless."

"I take my hat off to your skills at invention. Or would, if I had a hat."

"I contributed. I borrowed ideas from Wells. But Passepartout is the builder," Verne said.

Twain turned in his seat, looked at Passepartout, and nodded. "Thank you."

"Thank Mister Verne, he hired me for both my butler skills and my machine designing skills. But many people must be given credit for their discoveries from which we borrowed, and the machine itself was constructed with Mr. Verne's money, and a team of experts. I provided the blueprint and turned a few bolts myself, monsieur."

Ned was writing furiously. He held up the pad so Twain and Passepartout could see it.

PLEASE TO PAT EACH OTHER ON THE BACK LATER. MACHINES WITH UGLY OCTOPUSSIES STILL OUT THERE. WE ARE OUT THERE. WE ARE JUST ONE MORE INGREDIENT IN THE SOUP. DO WE HAVE SOUP ON BOARD?

Twain read this aloud so Verne could hear it.

"The seal is quite right; let us see if we can lose our enemies. See the device to your right, Samuel. I have one on my left."

"The mirror?"

"Ah, but it is arranged so that by looking into it you can see behind you. There are a series of mirrors alongside the craft, each feeding images into the other."

Twain looked. The Martian machines were running through the water toward them. And they were running fast. Twain could see at least five machines. White foam splashed up around the legs of the machines. One of them stumbled, fell, disappeared beneath the water, rose up again and continued its pursuit.

"This way, we can keep watch on what's behind us," Verne said. "The good thing is, they are behind us."

"They're catching up," Twain said.

"Yes," Verne said. "They are fast. But, can they manage the deep water?"

As if in answer, out of the heads of the machines came the hot rays. The beams hit all around Verne's racing craft, and where they hit the water steamed and hissed.

"They may not need to catch us," Twain said, looking into the relay mirror. "They can boil us in here like sardines in a can."

"I hardly think we would boil, sir," Passepartout said. "I think we would explode."

OKAY. THERE'S NO SOUP. BUT SARDINES WERE MENTIONED. DO WE POSSIBLY HAVE ANY OF THOSE? ANY KIND OF FISH? I'M WRITING HERE.

Twain patted Ned on the head. "Later, Ned. Later."

—◈◈—

They went far out fast and furious, and the water grew deep, and the silver machine rode up high on the waves and dipped and reared, and finally the walking machines began to fall deep. Pretty soon the water was up to the bulk of the machines, up to the windows that showed the tentacled aliens working at the controls as desperately as one armed paperhangers.

Then one machine went under and did not come up. Then another went down. Metal legs thrashed. One tried to rise. A wave took it and washed it back and under. It rose up again. All that could be seen was the top of the machine. The window. Green-gray heads behind it, flashing tentacles.

One of the beasts pressed its double anus against the glass. It and its companion Martian, its copilot, screamed and cursed. But the sleek silver craft darted over the waves, out of sight and sound of their grunts and sneezes, coughs and wheezes, and pretty soon the speedy boat, as Verne called it, was just a silver line, a shiny needle shooting through water, sewing up the ocean like a Neptunian tailor.

All of the Martian crafts floated to the surface. None was lost. They had crashed in the sea and had come out of the sea. They were prepared for that business. But they weren't ready to race across water. The could slide out of their "meteors" inside their little watertight air filled suits, click the machines together as fast as a kid could line up jacks. They could enter into their machines through their watertight, air-controlled hatches. And they could make the machines crawl across the bottom until they could stand tall and step on shore.

But that crossing the water bit, on the surface and fast, they had left that out of their plans. Someone had snoozed.

They stalked back to shore. The machines stood there on the sand. Tall, wet, and shiny. Inside the machines, the Martians, their critter faces pressed to their windows, looked out at the ocean and the world they intended to conquer, and they were seriously pissed off.

Nine

A Warm Sweet Day off the Coast of Spain, Followed by Disaster, And Further Surprise

Twain thought: Could he actually be back in Morocco, dozing, wine-sodden, out of his head, Huck on a shelf, shitted all over, fly-swarmed and dead?

He pinched himself.

Ouch.

Didn't seem that way.

—◦◦◦—

The craft went bumping over the waves. It made Twain sick at first, but in time, his stomach settled. There was the smell of the ocean being channeled through the top of the machine by a whirligig that pulled the air throughout, and in the beginning made the interior too cool and too strong with the smell of salt. But in time it became refreshing.

The stalking machines were long left behind, and now there was only the water and the jumping craft, bouncing up the waves and down them, in the ocean that was home to Gibraltar and the Pillars of Hercules. Just the thought of that made the historical-minded Twain happy. He could envision himself and his companions as ancient Greek heroes who had sailed this stretch of sea.

He tried to recall which heroes he had read about, which ones had sailed the sea on which they bounced.

Who was it?

Jason?

Odysseus?

Theseus?

All of the above?

He couldn't remember, but it was fun trying. And it was better than thinking about the machines. Twain was certain there were many more of them, and that they were spotted about the world. Had to be. If the meteors were in fact not meteors, but machines, craft from space, then there were many more. And had it not been for this fact, he would have enjoyed his trip.

That was nice to consider.

His life had been so miserable for so long, so lost without his wife and daughters, he had not considered the possibility of fun. Solace maybe, out of the contents of a bottle.

But fun?

Who would have thought? He actually felt good to be alive.

Of course, it was a partial kind of fun. The boat ride was nice. But what had gone on before, and might go on after, was bound to be less than fun.

Another snag was that Verne and Passepartout kept exchanging looks; Verne looking over his shoulder at the butler, his face scrunched up like fruit too long on the vine.

"What's wrong?" Twain said. "Something's wrong? Am I right? There's a snag. Right?"

"There is a snag that is small," Verne said. "Or, to say it another way. We are about to be snagged."

"How's that?"

"This craft, it is a prototype."

"So."

"So, it isn't designed to be...permanent."

"How's that?"

"The sides, the bolts, they are screwed in, okay, but not great."

"Why? Why would you do that?"

"Well," Verne said, looking at Passepartout, "we thought there were other things needed. So, the sides were designed to come loose easily, until certain changes were made inside. Designs, decorating."

"Decorating?"

Ned made a seal sound and twisted his mouth so that one side seemed to be wadded up. He slapped his pad, wrote, held it up. It said: I NEVER EVEN GOT TO TRY THE SHITTER.

Passepartout said, "It may hold long enough for us to reach land. Farther along, closer to Italy, that's our goal. But it's quite a ways, and though I think we'll arrive safely—"

The left side of the craft came off and water gushed up over the side. Passepartout said, "And maybe we shall not."

Ned wrote:

SHIT!

"To the rear," Verne said, "I shall hold its course. Hurry!"

Harnesses were unsnapped. Verne leaned the boat on its right side. More water crashed in from the left, rushed about their ankles. The top blew off and Twain and Passepartout and Ned were thrown to the rear.

Passepartout gestured to the circular couch, said, "Grab one end."

Twain struggled to his feet, did as he was told.

"Now push your end toward mine."

Twain did as he was told. The couch stretched as a partition came out of it, and it continued around until it clicked into the other end, forming a circle. Twain noted that there were thick rings placed strategically all around the top of the couch.

"The craft is losing its right side," Verne yelled.

Ned wrote on his pad: SNAPPY, SNAPPY, SNAPPY.

But no one was paying attention.

Passepartout climbed into the ring of the couch, sat on the cushioned seat, bid Twain and Ned to do the same. Twain helped Ned climb over, then they hoisted the cruiser into place. Passepartout took hold of the bottom edge of the couch and pulled. Thick wooden sections sprang out, snapped together, filled the gap.

"What good is a couch pulled into a circle?" Twain said.

Ned whistled and wrote. NOW IT HAS A BOTTOM. IT'S A BOAT.

Passepartout made no comment to either.

The right side of the boat shredded, just crunched up like an invisible hand had squeezed it. Verne righted it just in time to keep from being swamped. They were essentially jetting across the water now on a leaky, silver V.

The couch slid precariously to the left.

Passepartout lifted up one of the couch cushions. There was a box under it. He took out the box and set it in the center of the couch bottom he had made, opened it quickly. It was full of cables and the cables had snaps.

Passepartout snapped them into the rings around the top of the couch. The cables went from the couch, into the box, and in the box was something folded up. It was bright orange and of an odd texture.

"Stand back," Passepartout said, reaching into the box. He yanked something, a lever perhaps, and up jumped a balloon, hissing and filling and swelling up large. The cables struggled as they might yank the balloon back into the box.

"Jumping Horny Toads," Twain said. "All that was in that little box?"

"Sir," Passepartout yelled. "Master Verne. Please. It is time. It is past time."

The balloon was throwing off the boat's balance even worse, slowing it down, causing it to wobble. The back end dipped, the front end rose.

Verne unfastened his harness, careened and wobbled from his seat, lunged over the side of the couch onto its cushions.

"Grab your nuts, monsieurs" Passepartout said. "Master Verne, if you will assist me."

What happened next happened very quickly.

Verne leaned over one side of the couch, as did Passepartout, grabbed at something.

Twain peeked, saw on Verne's side that the couch was fastened to the floor by a cable and bolts, and there was a lift lever attached to the cable.

"One," said Passepartout, clutching a similar lever on the other side.

"Two," said Passepartout.

"Three," they said together.

Verne and Passepartout pulled the levers and the cables let go of the bolt.

They sprang to the heavens.

The motion was so hard Twain's neck was popped and he and Ned were nearly tossed out of the craft.

An instant later, beneath them, the boat wadded up and went to pieces in a million silver directions.

Out in the distance Twain saw an enormous swordfish jump, as if it were triumphant about the whole dang deal.

Ten

The Nature of the Device, Sailing Along, High Up, Full of Bread and Honey

"I can't believe it held as long as it did," Twain said. "With the balloon tugging, the wind, the speed."

"It may be a strange thing to say," Verne said, "considering it has come apart beneath us, but it was of an extremely sound design. Just wish we had not left the bolts loose."

"Yes, Passepartout. I do believe that furniture and decoration could have waited. But, alas. Millions of francs down the old shit hole."

"How does the balloon work?" Twain said. "It's not hot air."

"When the box was opened," Verne said, "the lever was pulled, and it was rushed full of the helium."

"Helium?"

"A gas. It works very good to make things float. Passepartout designed it so that a small compressor filled the balloon instantly."

"All of that helium out of that little box."

"A new design," Verne said. "A new way to condense helium. You will note the compressor in the bottom of the box."

"Amazing," Twain said.

"Yes," Verne said. "It is. The gas is very hard to come by, and it is very seriously compressed. Passepartout's design is years and years ahead of anything anyone else is doing."

"Thank you, sir," Passepartout said.

"You are quite welcome, my friend."

"It's certainly obvious that it is advanced," Twain said. "Like the boat."

Verne nodded, "Like the boat."

That got Twain to thinking.

"Is this a prototype too?" he asked.

"In a way, my friend, it is. Yes," Verne said. "We have never used it before, but, it is better constructed....But..."

"But what?"

"There is a problem."

"Figures. And that is?"

"It is not designed for the too long flight, you know. It will lose its buoyancy after a time."

"A short time?" Twain asked.

"Maybe not so short," Verne said.

"Maybe?"

"Who knows?"

"Great," Twain said. "We might as well shit on ourselves and call it lilac water."

The balloon kept rising and the sun was high and yellow and dripping over their balloon like a runny egg yolk. They sat in the shadow made by the balloon, and the wind carried them along, very fast, along the coast of Spain. Down below they could see the stalking machines.

Many of them.

Rays flashed. Farmhouses burned. They could see people running.

"Sweet Virgin," said Verne.

"I hope they don't look up," Twain said. "Those rays have quite a range."

They didn't look up.

Our heroes sailed along for some time, and then from under one of the cushions, Passepartout brought out a container of water, some food, bread and honey, utensils, and they ate and drank.

"How do we know we're going in the right direction?" Twain asked.

"That is one of the drawbacks," Passepartout said. "We do not. We have no navigational equipment on board."

"Oh, good," Twain said.

"And, for that matter, what is the right direction? Where are we going?"

"If we had a compass, at least, we could chart a course."

"If we could control the balloon's direction. We can not."

"No," Passepartout said. "We can not."

"Priceless," Mr. Twain said. "You don't have a plan?"

"My plan was to save our asses," Verne said. "Our asses are saved. At least for the moment."

"We won't go any higher, will we?" Twain said.

"No," Verne said. "Or, we shouldn't. And, in time, when land is near, we will leak the helium, bring us down. The important thing is we are away from those machines and our dissolving boat."

"I suppose," Twain said, finishing off a slice of bread with honey, "that is for the better."

In time they all lay about on the cushions and slept, Ned snuggled up close with Twain, his nose under Twain's chin.

The balloon, a giant tangerine in the sky, sailed on.

⟫◆⟪

The storm hit them like a fist.

It came down out of the sky like the howling vengeance of Zeus, wrapped itself around the balloon and tossed it this way and that, nearly throwing them all into the foaming ocean below. They managed from one of the containers under the couch cushions a large tarp that fitted almost snugly over the top of the basket. They fastened it there with the ties sewn to it, cowered under it, fearing any moment the balloon would be snapped from its cables. Or the basket would rip. Or the tarp would be torn off and they would be tossed like dice into the ocean.

The storm raged on and the balloon sailed on, making Ned so sick he stuck his nose out between tarp and basket and let loose with a stream of fish-smelling vomit.

The smell of long ago eaten fish came back to him on the wind, and strangely, made him a bit peckish.

When Ned was finished with this, he poked his head completely free of the tarp and looked out and tried to determine most anything there might be to determine. This proved no small feat.

He could not tell if they were directly over the water or high in the sky. The storm had become so furious it had balled up the world.

All Ned knew was that the ball he was in was a mixture of black and gray and bursts of lightning. And that in some manner, shape or form, they were between sea and sky, but if they were high or low, he could not determine.

He thought that if it were not for gravity, they could be flying upside down and he would never know it. He listened for the crash of his friend, the sea, but nothing.

There was just the howl and cry of the wind, the pounding rain and the strips of lightning that tossed about them as if they were spears being thrown at them from heaven.

How long before one hits, thought Ned? How long?

After a particularly ugly chain-reaction of hot lightning, so close the smell of ozone stuffed his nostrils like a rag, the wet-nosed seal pulled his head in under the tarp and lay down and tried to sleep to the toss and whirl of the basket. The sleep of the exhausted and the fearful overcame him as it did the others, and he spiraled down deep. In his dreams he was tossed into the sea, his home. The sea, though turbulent and frothed with storm, was smooth and silent beneath the waves. Full of fish. Great fish. And he took the fish, and he ate the fish, and finally he dreamed not at all.

The basket became a kind of bassinet, rocked by Mother Wind, rolled to the slam-pat-whammy of the cold, driving rain, the unmelodious lullaby given voice by the loud mouth of Captain Thunder and the snap crackle pop percussion of Old Man Lightning.

⊷⊶

Sometime while they slept, the storm ran its course. The sun poked out and it grew warm, finally hot. Twain rose up in a sweat and removed the tarp, folded it, put it away. The air was dry and heavy as chains.

None of the others moved. Ned lay on his back, his tail flipper in the air, his arm flippers folded over his chest. Twain thought the look on his face was one of satisfaction, as if he had just gobbled a tuna. Verne and Passepartout lay back to back like an old married couple.

Twain peeked over the side. A calm blue sea. He looked out, up and around. A calm, clear, blue sky and a huge yellow sun. But there was one peculiarity.

The sky seemed to have a rip in it. Like a painting of the sky that had been torn and pushed back together. Between the edges of the rip,

Twain thought he could see movement, but he couldn't identify it. The rip went from way on high, down to the sea, dropped into the horizon.

Peculiar, to say the least, Twain thought.

Cloud formation?

He couldn't decide. Gave it up.

They lived. That was the important thing. They lived.

Twain lay back down, surprised himself by falling asleep again. And he slept well.

There were flashes of light and waves of darkness in the crack in the sky. Shiny things. Dull things. Moving things. And then the crack narrowed.

Eventually it would be nothing more than a fine blue line.

Then that too would fade away.

But, before it did, something sailed out of the crack, onto the dark blue ocean below.

Black sails.

The Jolly Roger.

A large ship.

Pirates.

Part Two:

Extracted from the Diary and Journals of Ned the Seal

Eleven

The Mist, Ripped, the Terrifying Descent

Once upon a time I was a normal seal. This was before I was captured by Captain Bemo and given a great brain in this tin hat beneath this fine fez by none other than the infamous Doctor Momo on his secret island. My memories of this time are hazy. Once my brain power was increased, and I was given thumbs attached to my flippers, I became ravenous to learn, and read all the books that Captain Bemo had in the library aboard the *Naughty Lass,* and most of those on the island owned by Doctor Momo.

I did skip a number of his more graphic erotica books, as these tended to arouse me, and there were no female seals in my vicinity. You see, with the increase in my brain power, my sexual desires had increased as well. This waiting around for a female to be in heat, that was a bore. Sex for recreation. I want to state here and now that I'm for it. Long as the partners are willing, then why not.

But I have veered.

The books I loved the most were the ones the sailors owned and shared, the dime novels of Buffalo Bill and Wild Bill Hickok and Annie Oakley. Books about people I eventually met. I might also add that I read a book called *Frankenstein,* and I met the monster of that book, as well. He was really nice. The book only gave one side of the story, and it is certainly not well known, that Doctor Frankenstein died in a skating accident. This is how the monster told it, and I believe it. He seemed like a genuine sort of chap, and personally, I have no reason to doubt him.

The book, the biography of Frankenstein and his creation, takes quite a different slant, and gives the good doctor a different sort of demise, but as I said, I'm sticking with the monster's version. I got it straight from his dead lips, and he seemed as sincere as a hard-on.

Pardon my language, but I have been amongst a rough crowd.

Before the operation to make me smart, mostly what I remember is eating fish, mating with female seals (of course!), and avoiding sharks.

I do not like sharks. Not in the least bit. I have my reasons. One of which is that they ate a friend of mine. Or what was left of him. A talking head in a jar. He was the aforementioned famous Buffalo Bill and my hero, and they ate him. They tried to eat me too.(2)

They did bite me a lot, but I survived and I washed up on the shore that is called Spain and was rescued by none other than the famous writer, Mark Twain.

He is known primarily as a humorist, but since I have known him, he has not been that funny. He seems profoundly sad. I am sad too. I miss Buffalo Bill and Wild Bill Hickok and Annie Oakley and Sitting Bull, and there was also Cat. She was beautiful, like Annie, only she had once been a cat of some kind before Doctor Momo operated on her. He operated on himself as well. He gave himself a horse-size penis. Actually, he literally gave himself a horse penis. I assisted in the operation. He conducted it while awake, under a mild anesthesia. I think he liked a bit of pain. That was Doctor Momo's way.

Then again, that is all part of another story, contained in my diaries, and perhaps someday I will write of them, perhaps as fiction, perhaps as autobiography, perhaps as both.

But this time I'm telling you about, I was way up high in a balloon, and the day grew hot. Along we sailed, like a great orange moth, gliding with the wind, willy-nilly, with no particular place to go. We had escaped being killed by what Mr. Verne believed to be Martian invaders, and what were certainly large octopus looking things with two assholes. I saw the assholes when we came upon a dead one lying on the beach.

Anyway, we escaped from those eight armed sonsabitches by boat, then by balloon.

At first I found the whole thing quite the adventure. But after going

---

2. See *Zeppelins West* by Joe R. Lansdale (taken and adapted from dairies and journals by Ned the Seal plus speculation.)

through a horrible storm that made me think we would crash into the sea, and then to hope we would, I began to feel otherwise. Even when the storm passed, I grew anxious and felt restricted by the constructs of the balloon. Its interior was covered quite briskly and there was little to see on a second tour. You also had to shit over the side, and this is a precarious feat at best. And for me, a very heavy seal (which is not to say I am not trim, but I am a seal after all) with my ass dangling over the edge of a balloon while my companions moved to the far side to balance my weight, held my flippers so that my ass would not overload my body and send me dropping, it was, to say the least, an embarrassing situation.

I held it a lot. Which, I don't have to tell you, is not healthy.

With me in the balloon was Mr. Twain, the great writer, and Mr. Verne, also a great writer and an inventor. With him was his servant, friend, and fellow inventor, Passepartout. They were all real nice guys. It saddens me…Well, I will not go there. Not yet.

There was also limited food and water, and though, since the alteration of my brain, I can eat things like bread and honey with a certain delight, it is still not the same as fish, and beyond thinking about fish, which I must confess I am frequent to do, I was concerned about the state of our water. Already we had consumed half of the bottle Passepartout had produced from under a cushion, which was the lid to our food container.

And though he assured us that there was yet another container of the same, as well as slightly different foods in tins, stuffed beneath another couch cushion, I was still nervous about our odds. I confess it also passed through my mind, without any true warranty, I should hasten to add, that for three hungry men, a plump seal might began to look quite tasty after a few days with one's belly gnawing at itself.

This, of course, was most likely a silly consideration, though I did think that once I caught Passepartout giving me the once over, the way a butcher might eye a prize hog at a stock show (or so I've read in dime novels). But the heat, the boredom, the fear of death makes one think and consider all sorts of strange things, and even if I were to know for sure this passed through his mind, I forgive him. I forgive him too, because I sometimes saw the three of them as long white fish. And I thought about how those fish might taste. All I had to do was get them out of those clothes…Well, you see how it was.

Anyway, I thought about food a lot. I wondered if one of the tins inside the food container under the cushion had fish in it. If it did, I wondered if I could work the can opener, or cut into it with a pocket knife. I have thumbs, and I can do some things you wouldn't imagine a seal might do, but the use of really fine motor skills in the area of grabbing and such is not a specialty. I can pull my dick. I do that well. But I've discovered that this isn't an area of conversation that my companions wish to visit. They have, in fact, asked me not to do it while around them. Somewhere, in all my studies, perhaps due to my being around the foul and perverted Doctor Momo, I never learned that this whole yanking the tow line was a private matter.

Frankly, I still don't see the big deal.

I'm a seal. I don't wear britches. So, well, it's out there when I get ready for it to be. I get the urge, it pokes out.

I suppose, if I wore britches, I might not think about it as much.

But the bottom line is, up there in the air, hot, bored, frightened, I would have given my left nut for a big wet mackerel to slake my urges.

Or a sardine.

Or a tuna.

Or a salmon.

Most any kind of fish.

I looked over the edge of the balloon, down at all that water, begin to think about how much I would like to be there, all wet and sleek and diving down deep, hunting fish.

It even occurred to me to leap from the balloon, but I knew better. My brain had not been enhanced by Doctor Momo for no reason. It worked well, and I had studied much. I knew that from that height, were I to dive and hit the water, it would be the same as diving into a brick wall. I would be one splattered seal.

The wind died down, and the balloon slowed, and the day grew hotter and more miserable. For a seal without water it was murder.

Mr. Twain awoke, and seeing my distress, poured some of the remaining water on his hand and gave me a rubdown with it. It felt good, but its pleasurable sensations were brief. The sun dried me out quicker than a female seal's ass on a hot rock.

We drank a bit more of the water, ate some crackers from the second storage bin—just the wrong thing for such a hot, dry trip—but it's what we had, and tried to make the best of it.

Mr. Twain looked over the side of the craft, said, "Look, Ned, could that be land?"

A gray mist floated above the water and the mist was wide and thick, like a wool patch on the ocean, but at the edges of the mist we could see patches of what looked like shoreline.

"There must be land beneath that," Mr.Twain said. I would stake my royalties from *Tom Sawyer* on it. If I had royalties."

Mr. Twain stirred Mr. Verne and Passepartout from their slumber, took a look. It was generally agreed that it might be land.

As we floated nearer, it became more evident that it was indeed land. Misty and wet looking, but inviting, considering how hot we were up there. Outside of the mist, we could see for certain a sandy shoreline, a glimpse of trees. Still, it was quite contained in the mist, like a rock hidden in cotton candy, Mr. Twain said.

"Jules," Mr. Twain said. "How do we go down? We must go down."

Mr. Verne took in the situation immediately, looked up at the balloon and made a face.

"We seem to have made an error," he said. "There is in fact a release valve, but we unfortunately forgot to prepare a way to make it work from within the basket here, monsieur."

"What?" Mr. Twain said.

I wrote on my pad. WHAT? WHAT THE FUCK? THAT'S DUMB.

"I'm with Ned on this one," Mr. Twain said. "That was just plain old shit stupid."

"Actually," Mr. Verne said, "so am I. Not the shit stupid. But in agreement with Ned. I would like to remind everyone, though I provided the money for this device, I was not the one who designed the blueprints."

Passepartout cleared his throat. "You examined them."

"I am not an expert of the blueprints. I am not the builder."

"It is a prototype, my good monsieur."

"So it is," Mr. Verne said. "But now, what do we do, my good sir?"

Passepartout looked up, said, "Well, I fear there is but one thing to do."

"And that is?" Mr. Twain asked.

With a sigh, Passepartout said, "I'll need to climb up there and work the release valve. The problem is, when I climb up, it will distribute the weight in a not so good manner. Like when Ned takes the shit. You must arrange yourselves evenly about the basket."

I wrote:

ONE GOOD THING. I DON'T NEED TO GO RIGHT NOW.

"That is good, Ned," Mr. Twain said.

Everyone else agreed that was good.

"I can tell you this," Passepartout said, "don't let this device tip, or you will fall very far. I am going up now."

Passepartout took hold of one of the cables and said, "I'm going to put my foot on the edge here, so I can take hold of one of the cables to climb. Perhaps you should all move to the opposite side when I put my weight down and start to climb. But you will have to adjust as my weight is redistributed. You will need to do that instantly. And I advise strongly that you do not make with the fuck up."

Passepartout put his foot on the edge of the couch, or the basket as he referred to it, and indeed, the basket leaned in that direction, even with Twain, Verne, and myself on the opposite side. For a moment, I thought we were making with the fuck up.

Passepartout scooted up a cable, pulling with his hands, locking his feet around it for support. As the cable tapered to the center, and his position changed, the basket wobbled. We did our best to maintain proper distribution. Moving this way and that.

After what seemed like enough time for me to have eaten quite a lot of fish, he made it to the release valve, or just below it, where there dangled a hose and a clamp and a lever. He said, "I'm going to let out a bit of the helium. Be prepared for a sudden drop."

He pulled the lever and the hose opened. The hose whipped, and the helium gushed. The hose struck Passepartout so hard in the face, he let go of the cable.

And fell.

He fell to the center of the basket, and the basket slung back and forth, but remained centered. The balloon began to descend.

A little too quickly.

"Too much," Passepartout said. "I must fix it."

Passepartout, pushed upright, put a foot on the side of the basket, grabbed a cable, went up swift and nimble as a monkey this time. The basket shook like dice in an eager gambler's hand. (Note these similes. I read a lot and am quite proud of it. I am, after all, a seal.)

Passepartout fought to get hold of the flapping hose, and finally, after being struck on hands and face by the thing, which was popping about like an electrified eel, he nabbed it. (I like eel by the way. I have had it smoked and it is very good. I like it raw. They can shock you, some of them. You have to be careful. A little fishing tip.)

Passepartout closed off the lever with some difficulty, but maintained his position. He found that by locking his feet against the slanted cable, leaning into it, hanging onto the hose and using the other hand to release the lever, he could maintain a position on the cable and control the release of helium. Still, we were dropping a bit fast, and finally he closed it off.

Scootching down the cable to the basket, he said, "I think that we are low enough for the moment. It might be best that we acquire the lay of the land, and then plan our descent a bit more precisely. Otherwise, to put it bluntly, we might end up with the pointy top of a tree up our asses."

"That wouldn't be good," Twain said. "I like your suggestion."

I wrote:

IT WOULD HAVE TO BE SEVERAL POINTY TOPS TO STICK IN ALL OUR ASSES.

"You are right, of course," Passepartout said.

The descent had created a new problem. Down there was a humid mist, and it rose up and surrounded us. We couldn't really see what was below us, only above us, and up there was the bright orange balloon and the hot blue sky, and as we dropped down into the mist, like drugged bug specimens in cotton, the sky and the sun began to disappear.

It was while I was looking up that I saw something moving through the mist. A big, dark dot. And the dot was growing, descending from on high. And then I saw what it was. I grabbed my pad and wrote.

LOOK UP! A BIG FUCKING BAT, I THINK.

Twain looked up. "Oh, shit."

Mr. Verne said, "My God, a pterodactyl."
I JUST SEE THE BAT.
The beast attacked the balloon.

———————

The creature, bat, pterodactyl, winged snake, whatever, was diving at a rapid rate. Its mouth was open and it had as many teeth as a barracuda.

Perhaps the oddness of the balloon, its bright color (can birds see color? I can since the operation , but before, I saw in black and white) had annoyed the bird. I know bright orange annoys me. I am not overly fond of lavender, either. And there are some shades of green I find irritating.

"Shoooo, shoooo!" Verne screamed at the beast, but we were, as they say, shit out of luck.

The beast hit the balloon with its mouth open; its fangs tore at the balloon. There was a sound like a whale spouting water through his blowhole. The blast of helium hit the creature full in the face and knocked it back.

It screeched, whirled and wheeled in midair, went up into the higher reaches of the mist, out of sight, and at the same time we lurched and wheeled and the basket slung us all over the place.

We were nearly thrown out. Our water and much of our supplies were tossed, and the water canister grazed my head and bounced into Mr. Twain, which made him cuss, and then I was hardly aware of anything.

We clutched whatever we could grab as if it were life itself, and in a sense, it was. The basket dropped out from under us at times, then snapped back under our feet (in my case, I use that euphemistically), as we were jerked about by the wheezing, cable tugging balloon.

After what seemed like enough time to have had a great meal of fish and a squid, the balloon became less radical in its movements, but more determined in its descent. We would not be choosing our landing area now, and I thought about what Passepartout had said about a pine tree up the ass, found myself tightening my sphincter muscles.

I chanced a look over the side of the basket, saw mist, and then poking up from the mist, what Passepartout had suggested might be there, and what I feared.

The tip of a tree.

Though, at that moment in time, I couldn't tell if it was in fact a pine.

Twelve

Ned's Journal Continues with a Lost Land, Seal Nookie, Fresh Fish and Strange Circumstances

And so we fell, and the tip of the pine (for so it proved to be) jammed through the bottom of the basket, poked right through the wooden floor of our craft until it seemed to rise in front of us like a decorative parlor plant. Then suddenly the pine expanded as the branches, momentarily trapped by the floor of our craft, sprang back into position. Our vessel burst apart, except for the leaking balloon, which still hovered above us, whistling helium out of itself like a slow fart from a fish-filled seal, unlike myself who was fishless and fartless.

(We seals make a lot of fart references. It is not considered rude to fart when you are a seal. Though, I will say that what a walrus passes for gas can be considered very rude in most kinds of company, mixed or otherwise.)

———⊷∘⊶———

We found ourselves clinging to the limbs of the pine, the shattered pieces of our former airborne ride raining all around us, and slowly above us the bright balloon lost its special kind of air, withered like a geriatric woman's breasts, fell down over us and the top of the great tall tree, concealing us in a rubbery darkness.

Carefully, we climbed from beneath the balloon, clutching at limbs.

It was decided that the others would go to the ground, and that I, being a poor climber, would wait amongst the pine limbs, draped over them like a lumpy rug.

They went down to search for the scattered supplies, and in time, a metal box that had been in a compartment under one of the cushions was recovered. There were all manner of things inside. A pistol. Ammunition. Flares. A First-aid kit. A large hacking instrument. A kerosine lantern wrapped tight with cotton and cloth. A corked bottle of kerosine, also wrapped in cotton and cloth. And, for me, most importantly, a rope.

Mr. Twain climbed up to help me, which for a man his age was remarkable. He removed his coat and shirt and managed a rig for me out of them, so the rope wouldn't cut into me too badly. I was also protected by my vest. The rope was attached to me and dropped over a strong limb. Below, Verne and Passepartout helped lower me down.

While Mr. Twain restored himself to his shirt, and I rubbed my chest with my flippers, trying to dispel some of the rope pain, for in spite of shirt and vest, I had been temporarily indented, Passepartout clambered monkey-like back up the tree, slipped under the balloon. Using his pocket knife to cut the rubber around the cables loose, he managed, with much effort, to push the balloon free of the pine. It dropped to hang in the boughs of another tree.

On the way down, Passepartout, in continued monkey-like fashion, swung over to that tree, and with a bit of effort kicked the balloon loose of that tree. It fell in a flutter and a crash to the forest floor, not far from where we stood.

When Passepartout was on the ground, Mr. Verne said, "And why, may I ask, did you bother with that business?"

"Because we may need shelter," Passepartout said. "I thought the balloon might make quite a good one. At least for keeping the rain off. From the lushness of this island, it is my guess it rains frequently."

Mr. Verne thought about that for a moment. "Of course. Sam, what do you think?"

"What's to think," Mr. Twain answered. "He is as right as rain, so to speak. Thing I'm worried about at the moment is food. What little we had, those crackers, got knocked all over this island or jostled out at sea."

"Tubers," Passepartout said. "There are quite a few of those about. We can dig those up. And we do have matches."

"And, with the sea nearby," Mr. Verne said, "we should be able to wash them and clean them. We might even catch some fish."

"We have quite a fisherman right here," Mr. Twain said, nodding at me.

I pushed my chest out with pride.

A fish would have been good right then.

Several would have been better.

Fish are good to eat and they give me solace.

Like masturbation, they relax me.

Did I mention that I think it is okay to masturbate?

"It is my guess that Ned would very much like to dip himself in the sea," Mr. Verne said.

I wrote on my pad:

THAT'S RIGHT. I WOULD. I LIKE THE OCEAN AND SLOW SWIMS AND EATING FISH.

"What a strange place," Mr. Twain said. "Visibility on the ground is good, but the mist, it hangs high up, and from what we could see, almost to the edge of the beach. Can you explain it, Jules?"

"Perhaps the foliage, a number of large beasts. They breathe air in, but they breathe out something quite different, like humans. It maybe makes the mist."

"That doesn't work for me," Mr. Twain said, "but it's better than anything I can come up with it."

I wrote:

IT COULD BE MAGIC.

"I do not believe in magic," said Mr. Verne.

"What we don't understand, even if there is an explanation, might as well be magic. So, I'm with Ned. Magic it is."

We decided to break into two parties. Mr. Twain and I were given the task of taking me to the sea for a dip, as well as a search for food or water. Since we could hear the crashing of the ocean from where we were, there was little chance we might get lost. There was, however, no true trail that we could see, so we assumed our journey might be a tedious one.

It was made a lot more pleasant than it might have been for my belly, but for the discovery of the cruiser. It was popped out to full size, and Mr. Twain and I climbed on board. I worked the switch, and with a hiss it rose off the ground.

"Seems no worse for wear," Mr. Twain said.

"We'll start building a shelter," Mr. Verne said. "Maybe recover some of the food that was dropped out of the balloon basket. You might want to be back here before dark, however, considering what attacked us up there, no telling what there is in the depths of these woods, or even along the beach."

"Daylight won't protect us," Mr. Twain said.

"No, but at least you can see it coming," Mr. Verne said.

"Good point," Mr. Twain said.

"There is the large knife...the machete from the survival box," Passepartout said. "You may have to make way for the cruiser. Take it."

Mr. Verne opened the box, took out the machete and gave it to Mr. Twain.

I felt Mr. Twain and I had gotten, as Buffalo Bill might say, the better end of the stick. Our task, daunting as the undergrowth might be, was child's play compared to finding a few dirty crackers strewn about the forest floor, and possibly a water bottle.

We started out, and it was a rough go. Limbs smacked us, and several times Mr. Twain had to get out of the cruiser and hack us a path. Tired and wheezing, he would gratefully mount the cruiser again, and off we would go. This was our method for some time, inching our way through the jungle, me following the smell of the sea. And let me tell you, dear readers, that smell, to me, was as fine as any whiff of French perfume.

After some time, we burst out of the thick growth and moved beyond the edge of the mist, sweaty and dirty, onto the white sand shore and the sight of waves crashing fast and furious in rolls of foam.

"I wonder where we are," Mr. Twain said. "We must be off the coast of Spain or Italy...But which island is this? It seems unlike any I'm aware of in the Mediterranean."

I took my pad and marker and wrote:

THE WIND WAS HIGH. WE SAILED FAST. WE COULD BE ANYWHERE.

Mr. Twain nodded. "You're right. We could be anywhere."

I stared at the sea and licked my lips.

"Go," Mr. Twain said. "I intend to dampen up, myself."

I pushed my pad against my vest, removed my fez, waddled to the water and went in. It was beauty itself. For now I was sleek and fast and part of the great sea, and in that moment, I was no longer Ned, but just a seal, a creature of instinct and muscle. I dove deep, and swam far, seeing silver flashes of fish. A free lunch, if I could catch it.

And I could.

I ate my fill. It was delightful to have a belly full of fish. I decided to catch more, take them to shore so that they might be carried back. But then, as I rose out of the water, looked back, saw Mr. Twain stripped of his clothes, frolicking in the sea, I smelled something that made my whiskers twitch and my flippers flip.

Seal nookie.

I might have been civilized by a better brain, by experience and books, but when that smell hit my nose, I was nothing more than a horny seal with a little pickle dick hard as a coral reef.

I found her sunning on a rock. Her and about fifty other seals. She flirted with me a bit, finally gave me her rear. I mounted her. And then it was over and she was gone, back into the sea with the others.

I had no real urge to follow them. There was no real regret when they swam out of sight. I was no longer of their world, but I felt empty. I had mated, but it had been nothing more than that. A cheap, sordid moment on a warm rock. I was embarrassed. I hoped, that from where Mr. Twain was, he could not have identified that it was me. Though with the metal cap on my head, shining in the sunlight, it was quite possible that during my moment of digression I was visible, hunkering up there on the rock, wetting my wick like a common beast.

Embarrassed, I entered the water again, found a large fish, nabbed it by the head in my teeth, and swam back to shore with it.

Unfortunately, I ate it before landfall. So, I had to go back and catch another. Luckily, it was an even larger specimen.

I dropped it on the sand just as Mr. Twain was coming out of the sea, nude, dripping, and tired. I made a noise, and he saw me and my fish, and smiled. It was good to see him smile. In that moment, I think he must have felt pretty good. The sea is such a revitalizer of spirit.

I went back into the sea. Went three times. Each time I came back with another fish. Now there were four fish. All were rather large. I had lived up to the praise Mr. Twain had given me.

Mr. Twain dressed while I replaced my pad and pencil, pushed my hat on my head.

We started back, and as we went, the sun dipped down and turned a fiery red. It fell toward the sea, and made a flaming fruit on the far side of the ocean, then melted slowly into the sea. It would have been a strange and beautiful sight, had we been returning to Mr. Verne's beach house, but out here, not knowing where we were, it was hard to feel jovial, and that mist above and beyond, hanging there hour after hour, gave me a sensation of creepiness that made my slick seal hair stand up like porcupine quills, made the long whiskers on my face twitch involuntarily.

"I believe we have let this beautiful sunset keep us from doing what Jules suggested. Be back before dark."

There was, however, still a slash of red in the sky, and we used it to guide us as we climbed onto the cruiser and started back.

Things were good in that moment, but my experiences had taught me one sure thing.

Never feel too secure. Life always has a loose sphincter somewhere, and it will let go when you least expect it, drench you from head to toe. Or, in my case, nose to tail.

Thirteen

Ned's Journal Continues: Back at Camp, Shelter and a Fish Dinner, a Cry in the Night

We were all heroes that day. We had all done well.

Mr. Twain and I returned with fish. Mr. Verne and Passepartout had built a shelter out of the balloon. And it was a nice one. They had cut strips of rubber from it, stretched it over limbs and drooped in on two sides and at the back. Only the front of our shelter was open.

They had found a fistful of crackers, a water bottle, and not twenty feet from where we had crashed, a small spring feeding a narrow, slow-flowing creek.

They had also gathered wood, and using matches from the supply box, we had a fire, and soon, cooking fish. I confess that I did not mention that I had already eaten many fish. I like fish, you see. I like them raw just fine. But cooked is all right. If you have the patience. Having already eaten several gave me the patience.

For the moment we had shelter, water, food, and companionship, and by eating my piece of fish cooked, I could perhaps appear a bit more sophisticated.

It was bad enough I had been driven by my baser instincts to mount a seal I didn't even know, but I had also stuffed my belly like a glutton, thinking not once of my hungry partners. I was grateful that in the end I had had enough ambition to go back into the deeps and bring out dinner for everyone else.

After dinner, Mr. Twain, full of fish, having had a drink at the stream, began to talk, and he was very funny. He gave two of his after dinner speeches, then recited a very funny story about how it was to go the barber, and finally he quoted aloud from an article he had written called "The Literary Offenses of James Fennemore Cooper."

Mr. Verne was howling, and I was rolling about on the ground, the both of us having read, or attempted to read, the long-winded, aimless tales by Mr. Cooper. Passepartout just grinned. He had not read the stories.

Except for the fact that by having read the Cooper tales we were familiar enough with them to enjoy Mr. Twain's oral article with an expulsion of great soul-satisfying mirth, I am of the opinion that Passepartout was, in fact, the luckiest of we four. For unlike us, he had not had the original pain of trying to digest and make sense of the stories.

After a time the cooking fire, which was too warm for comfort anyway, burned low, and the conversation turned to females. Mr. Twain told us of the great love of his life, his wife, Olivia, and Mr. Verne told us of his life and loves, but Passepartout was a veritable rabbit packed with sexual adventures. Many of them harrowing and funny, and, I must confess, stimulating.

I, having only a small erasable pad to write with, and being bashful, did not feel driven to try and sort out dim memories of my matings with the female clan before my brain enhancement. Nor did I wish to recall the earlier events of the day, desperately hunching a warm seal on a warm rock in the ocean.

—◆—

Finally, after being coated in water from the creek by Mr. Twain, (he carried it to me in the water bottle that had been found) I turned in, as did the others. Our beds were soft piles of leaves, the air was warm, our bellies full. Soon, we were fast asleep.

This was our life for several days. Eating fish that I caught, and the roots that the others dug, drinking from the spring and telling tales into the night.

At that moment in time, I felt that our lives were good ones. In Europe, probably all over the world, Martian invaders were wreaking havoc, and here we were, relatively cozy, no immediate worries other than me easily catching a few fish, the others digging up tubers like lazy bears, sitting around the campfire at night telling tales, and me in the dark, when they weren't looking, pulling the old tuber. I suspicion they might be pulling tubers as well, but I felt it impolite to ask or lie awake listening.

It was quite the wonderful life.

And it made us all feel guilty.

The lot of us wanted to return to Europe, and see what we, as earthlings, could do to combat this ugly Martian menace. It was my opinion, that if they could be stopped, they might be edible. There could turn out to be a really positive side to the whole thing. A lot of people, and at least one seal, could be well fed on the bodies of those Martians.

After all, it wasn't like eating human or seal flesh.

They were just big octopi, or octopussies. Whatever the term might be.

Kill them. Stop them. Eat them. Sounded like a plan to me.

⊰·⊱

I don't know exactly how long we lived like this, because I lost track of time after seeing the sun go down seven times, and it is my guess it may have gone down another seven times before fate, as I originally suggested it would, let its sphincter go.

We were asleep, having had a particularly entertaining night of talk and excessive food (I caught a lot of fish that day, not counting the ones I ate while at sea, and we all ate an excessive amount of cooked tubers), and I was dreaming of a fish the size of Jonah's whale when we were startled awake by a cry in the night.

It came from some distance, but it was loud.

"It sounds like someone in pain," Mr. Twain said, rising up on one elbow.

"Or someone who is very angry," Mr. Verne said.

"Or both," Passepartout said.

"Could it be one of those sky monsters?" Mr. Twain said.

"It could be anything, Samuel," Mr. Verne said. "But what did it sound like to you?"

"What I said originally. Someone in pain."

"Precisely."

"Since it isn't any of our business," Mr. Twain said, "I suppose we will check into it."

Mr. Verne was already up, slipping on his shoes. "I think that we must."

Mr. Verne took the pistol from the box, made sure it was loaded, then dropped the box of ammunition in his loose coat pocket.

Mr. Twain picked up the machete, and Passepartout found a heavy but not too long limb to carry as a club. I carried with me only my wits.

I doused myself in spring water as a refresher, and soon as Mr. Verne brought the collapsible cruiser into full service, I, along with the others mounted it. Lighting the lantern from the box, fastening it to the front of the cruiser, we started out, Mr. Verne at the controls.

<hr />

The sound, which was now more of a groan than a cry, continued, and we pushed on through the dense foliage in pursuit of it.

A part of me thought this a foolish idea, but another part of me, and I almost said the human part of me, for I had been changed considerably by the introduction of a larger brain and by the friendship of others and the addition of thumbs, which was the device that allowed me to pull, rather than lick (on occasion, I still do that) the old tuber, knew we had to give it examination. It might be someone in pain, in need of our assistance. And a gentleman did not sit on his hands, or flippers, when there was a cry of distress.

Or it might be a scary monster that wanted to eat us. And in that case, sitting on your hands, or flippers, is appropriate.

The night was not very bright because of the mist that surrounded the island, but the full moon, like a greasy doubloon seen through cheesecloth, provided far more light than one would have thought possible in a land of mist, and, of course, we had our lantern.

Still, it was not high noon, and we went along, bumping up against trees, having to get out and clear brush (actually, I didn't get out; I would have slowed us down considerably), looking this way and that for a trail.

Finally, we decided it was best to just head to the beach, listen from there, and then find our way back in. Trying to thread our way to the cries in the dark was impossible. But, out on the beach, once we located the cries, perhaps we could ride directly to them. It was my surmise that the sounds were not too deeply in the woods, but along the edge.

We found the trail that Mr. Twain and I had cleared, and once on that, our time picked up. As we neared the beach, we realized that the sound had been coming from there all along, not the woods at all. Something about the island, the trees, the crashing sea, had made the source and distance of sound hard to determine.

Now, we realized they were originating somewhere down on the beach, and that they were moving away from us. Eventually, we came out of the forest and hovered over the sand.

There in the fuzzy moonlight, we could see a horde of footprints. Some of them shoed, some bare. Among them were a few huge prints that did not appear human. There was also the sign of something large being dragged, like a sled. A very big sled. This dragged thing had mashed down many of the odd, nonhuman appearing prints, but the few of those prints that were visible were well indented, which, from having read Buffalo Bill's adventures, I knew meant that what-ever was on the other end of those feet was large and heavy.

"What do you make of it, friends?" Mr. Verne asked.

Mr. Twain climbed out of the cruiser, bent down and touched the big track.

"Well, if this was a Fennemore Cooper novel," Mr. Twain said, "we could not only determine what made this print at a glance, we could probably tell its age, hat size, and the length of its dong. Then we could dig it out, harden it in about five minutes by blowing on it, then ride about in it on the ocean like a boat, having swollen it to thirty times its size by a piece of bullshit esoteric Indian lore."

"You do not like this Fennemore Cooper's work, do you, my friend?" Passepartout said.

"Nope," Twain said.

"I am no tracker, no Hawkeye," Mr. Verne said, "but what we can do, since there are tracks most everywhere, is follow them."

"What if we do catch up with them?" Mr. Twain said.

Mr. Verne paused. "Might I suggest extreme caution."

"That's how I'd play it," Mr. Twain said.

"It would be smarter to ignore the whole thing," Passepartout said.

About that time there came a long loud cry that trailed off into a horrid groan.

Mr. Twain had risen from examining the track. He said, "Perhaps. But can any of us ignore that?"

"I can not, sir," Mr. Verne said. "Though, perhaps, before this night is over, I will wish that I had ignored it."

"Let's get to sneaking," Mr. Twain said.

Fourteen

Ned Passes Gas, an Incredible Discovery

We had not gone far before the fish I had eaten earlier went to work on me. I love fish, but like most seals, it gives me gas. And it's a foul gas, I might add. But I'll not discuss it in detail, because it has been mentioned before and humans seem somewhat reticent to talk about the natural processes of their bodies.

"Ned," Mr. Twain said, "you keep that up, and you can get out of the cruiser and waddle along."

I wrote on my pad and pushed it around where he could see it. SORRY, MR. TWAIN. I CAN'T HELP IT. SOMETIMES, IF YOU EAT MORE FISH IT WILL SETTLE THE STOMACH. WE COULD PAUSE HERE WHILE I GRAB A SNACK IN THE SEA.

"No time for that, Ned."

SORRY. OF COURSE, YOU ARE RIGHT. BUT IT WOULD TAKE ONLY A MOMENT.

Mr. Twain ignored me, which I suppose was best. We cruised along the beach, and sometimes we rode over the waves as they crashed against the sand. I loved the sound of the waves, the smell of the sea, its white foaming thunder broken only by the occasional moans or cries of that which had awakened, and now, guided us.

As we traversed the beach, the shoreline narrowed, and the jungle trees pushed out closer to the ocean. They were scrawny there, and pale from the leaching of the salt spray.

We could see where whatever it was that had been dragged, had in fact, been pulled into the water, and then around the outcrop of jungle, back onto where the beach became wide again.

Beyond that, we saw the blaze of a large fire. It gave off a great orange glow. And now we could identify what had been dragged. It

was high and dry and parked between a couple rows of widely spaced palm trees. It was a ship. A large wooden ship. And, not far off shore, in a kind of cove was another ship. Its black sails were trimmed. On a high mast a Jolly Roger floated in the sea breeze and flapped like a wag's tongue.

What swarmed over the beached ship and the shore around it made our jaws drop. They could only be described as pirates. Of the yo-ho-ho variety. Appearing to be of an age long lost. They looked as if they could have stepped out of some of the old pirate books I had read.

I was so shocked, and secretly delighted, I thought I might shit myself.

And they were jubilant pirates at that. Leaping and cavorting, drunk as flies in a barrel of cider, cutlasses waving about or strapped to their sides, belts stuffed with old fashion cap and ball pistols, or brandishing old-style rifles about, they danced around the fire to the crude stylings of an old squeeze box, pushed and pulled by a large man in a wide-brimmed hat. His leg looked to be nothing more than a peg of wood.

There was something else. Something large amongst the palm trees. Something I could not identify, but something that moved.

The noise we had been following, the cries, they came from this large thing's quarter. And there was another thing, a screeching sound, and the slash and pop of what sounded like a dozen whips. And when they popped, the thing in the dark cried.

"I suggest," Mr. Twain said, "we ride up in those woods there, and sneak around. I got a feeling being seen head on might not work out to well for us."

"Oui," Mr. Verne said.

—◦◦◦—

So we used the cruiser to glide into an opening in the jungle, began making slow progress through gaps in the trees toward the camp. The jungle rose up dramatically from where the beach had widened and this positioned us high up and amongst the greenery, looking down.

We climbed down from the cruiser, collapsed it and leaned it against a tree. Then we got low and crawled along on the ground until we were at the edge of the trees, up above them on an overlook built over the centuries by sand being pushed in from the shore and the sea bottom. It smelled very fishy. Very nice.

I did not like crawling on my stomach however. There were rocks in the sand and they cut me a bit.

Down below we could hear their laughter and yelling, the cries and groaning of that which was in the shadows, and of course, that miserable music from the squeeze box. Some were even singing pirate songs. Yo-ho-ho and a bottle of rum stuff. It was all quite off-key, I might add.

Now we were close enough that we could identify (I don't know if that is the proper word) the great shape from which the cries emitted, the great shape that was the target for the whips.

It was an ape.

Sort of.

The beast was forty feet tall if it was a foot, and very broad. There were chains around its neck, wrists and ankles. A sort of grinding machine had been put on the beach, something from the pirate ship no doubt, and it had a wheel on it, and it was turned by the ape, grinding...whatever...in the moonlight.

I could see the name of the beached vessel written its side—*Der Fliegende Hollander.* Sitting with their backs against the ship were a number of bedraggled people. A rope ran along the side of the ship, from bow to stern, and other ropes had been attached to that rope, and in turn the people had been fastened to those. They looked as dejected as pet pigs that had been decided on for dinner.

Then, I almost cried out. For I recognized two of the captives.

The Sioux warrior and visionary, Sitting Bull, and the black-haired beauty, Cat—her name being the source of her origin—were among the prisoners.

I wrote:

I KNOW TWO OF THE CAPTIVES. THEY ARE MY FRIENDS. SITTING BULL AND CAT. I THOUGHT THEY WERE DEAD. WE WERE IN THE *NAUGHTY LASS* AND IT SUNK. I THOUGHT THEY, LIKE BUFFALO BILL'S HEAD, WERE EATEN BY SHARKS. BUT, LIKE ME, I SEE THEY SURVIVED.

"I'll be damned," Mr. Twain said.

ME, TOO. WHAT CAN WE DO?

Mr. Twain patted me on the head, said, "Hold your water. Yes, I recognize Sitting Bull now. From photographs. But there is another Indian down there. See the braid? Do you recognize him or any of the others?"

NO.

I turned my attention once again to the great ape, who was working at turning that odd wheeled device, going round and round to the snap and pop of pirate whips.

The beast pushed at the wheel by grabbing onto the bar to which it was chained, putting his back into it.

Around and around went the wheel, and I could discern now that the wheel was some kind of crushing device, and that pirates were feeding something into a space beneath it, and that when the wheel turned, the stuff was crushed, the residue forced through a pipe, into a barrel, beneath which was a hot fire.

Twain sniffed. "Mash," he said. "They're making some kind of liquor with a crude crushing device they've rigged. It looks to be a type of cane they're crushing. Like sugar cane."

"Now it is my turn to be damned," Mr. Verne said.

"Probably discovered the cane on the island, and are as happy as clams about it," Mr. Twain said. "My guess is they were spending time here, resting up, drinking, and they spotted this ship and went out to take it. And did. Had this ape pull it to shore. My guess is, like the cane, they discovered him on the island. Makes sense considering what we've seen here. That great beast that brought us down, for example."

"It's easier to scuttle a ship that way," said Passepartout. "Having it on shore."

"But pirates?" Mr. Verne said. "These people look out of their time. That ship. Both ships. Their clothes. The cutlasses, the cap and ball pistols. Most odd."

"That ship, the beached one, or the one docked off the island, could be our way out," Mr. Twain said. "Provided we could rescue a crew from the pirates. I, for one, couldn't sail a rowboat. Now, if it were a steam craft, and had a paddle wheel, we would be in luck."

"Since there is no paddle wheel," Mr. Verne said, "might I suggest another plan."

"Okay?" Mr. Twain said.

"I didn't say I had one," Mr. Verne said. "I said I suggest we have another. Anyone?"

Mr. Twain said, "I suppose there is only one thing to do, and that's wait. Perhaps, if those reprobates drink enough grog, tire of making more, they will go to sleep. Then and only then can we slip down and free them."

"Making instant grog," Passepartout said. "Without aging, that is bound to be nasty."

"The cane is probably old, maybe even decayed," Twain said. "That way, it ripens almost instantly. It may not be fine liquor, Passepartout, but enough of it will get you drunk. And there is little doubt in my mind that is their ultimate goal."

"Most uncivilized," Passepartout said.

Fifteen

Ned's Journal Continued: a Daring Plan, a Surprise Ally, Bull Goes Crazy

As we watched, the stocky peg-legged pirate we had spotted before came well into view. His wide-brimmed hat hung over his head like a black cloud and a nasty looking pigtail wormed from the back of his head and was draped over the shoulder of his filthy blue coat like some sort of horrid little beast that had died in its sleep. A cutlass dangled at his side. He had a crooked dagger in his broad belt, as well as two old single shot cap and ball pistols. In the firelight his face looked rough, as if it had been used to sand flooring then hosed down and left out in the sun to dry.

He said something to the crowd that we couldn't hear, and a cheer went up. As we watched, a barrel was rolled out, tapped, and the pirates began to fill whatever they could find with the liquid, drink it faster than I gobble fish, and believe me, I gobble pretty quick.

"All we can do," Mr. Twain said, "is wait until they're so drunk they pass out, then maybe, we can slip in, free the prisoners, and run away, back to our camp and hide."

"What about the boat plan?"

"That's plan B, if plan A goes real well. Plan A never goes real well."

"I hate to suggest it," Passepartout said, "but perhaps the better part of valor is to watch out for ourselves. We can not do for us, let alone many others."

I wrote: BULL AND CAT ARE MY FRIENDS. I MUST SAVE THEM. WITH OR WITHOUT THE REST OF YOU.

"I am sorry to have said such a thing," Passepartout said. "I was wrong to think it. It just came out."

"You were merely saying what all of us, with perhaps the exception of Ned, are thinking," Mr. Twain said, patting Passepartout's arm. "Of course, we will all do what we can, Ned. We know what we must do. But we must be cautious. There's no use going off half-cocked. That will not help us one little bit. We rest here, wait until they are blind drunk."

I lay on my back beside Mr. Twain on the ground, brooding. It is uncomfortable for me to lie on my back like that, but I brood better that way.

"Uh, what are they doing now?" Mr. Verne said.

I rolled over on my belly for a look.

A couple of the pirates went over to the trotline that held the row of prisoners, picked one, a smallish brute of a man, cut him free of the line, brought him over to the pirate who appeared to be their captain, the one with the greasy pigtail and the wide-brimmed hat.

The Captain, as I will call him, looked at the man and laughed. He said something, and the man said something back, dropped to his knees and begged. I couldn't hear him beg, for which I am grateful, but begging was what he was doing. That was obvious.

He was pummeled by a couple of the pirates, stripped of his boots and clothes. When it was over, he lay naked and bloody on the sand.

While this had been going on, ropes were attached to two young palm trees, and with all the pirates pulling, the trees were bent over to where the tops almost touched the ground and they crossed against one another. They were held that way by the horde of straining pirates.

"What are they doing?" Mr. Verne said.

"I don't know," Mr. Twain said. "But I don't like it."

The brutish looking man was swiftly bound to the trees in such a way that one arm and one leg were tied firmly to each tree with thick rope. A small barrel of pitch was produced from somewhere, and with a stick a tad of it was scooped, touched to the tip of the man's penis. This was set on fire. The man screamed so loud I thought I was going to suck my asshole up through the top of my head. Then the pirates let go of the trees.

It happened with a snap and a whoosh. The man's body was torn in half, launched high in two directions. The flaming dick went to the right, a little red blur that sailed way out into the ocean, dropped down like a miniature falling star into the water.

A cheer went up from the pirates.

I looked down at Cat and Bull. In the light from the moon, which was clear of mist out there on the beach, and the flickering of the fire-light, Cat looked nervous as a cat might look. She certainly knew that a very special fate was probably in store for her. A plaything to the pirates, and then the trees.

The others on the trotline looked nervous as well. A couple were actually trembling. Bull was the only one who didn't look in the least bit bothered. He looked as if he might be thinking of supper, hoping for boiled dog.

Watching, knowing what fate might be in store for my two friends, knowing others might die, made me sick to my stomach, and for the first time that I can ever recall, at least for a few minutes, I did not think of fish.

There was a pause, more grog was drunk, then another victim was picked from the trotline. The same ritual occurred, with the same horrible results.

WE MUST DO SOMETHING, I wrote.

Mr. Twain said, "We are four against many. There must be forty pirates. We have one gun. We must wait."

GIVE ME THE GUN. I WILL GO DOWN THERE.

"You are brave, little seal," Mr. Verne said. "No doubt. But if you wish to help your friends, you must wait until the pirates sleep."

WHAT IF MY FRIENDS ARE TIED TO THE TREES AND SET ON FIRE AND SHOT IN TWO DIRECTIONS. THEN HOW DO I HELP THEM? WHAT OF THE OTHERS? I DON'T KNOW THEM, BUT ARE THEY NOT HUMAN? ARE WE NOT HUMAN? EXCEPT, OF COURSE, I'M A SEAL.

"And as humans," Mr. Twain said, "we must know our limitations. If we all die, we will have accomplished nothing."

I started to write again, but felt suddenly fatigued. I did not like it, but they were right. I lay down on my belly and waited.

Two more victims were sent sailing from the trees, but fortunately, neither was Cat nor Bull.

After a time, the pirates bored with the whole matter, drank more, and got into fights with one another. There was even a stabbing, which resulted in a death right there on the shore. Or a near death. The poor man was gutted, and with his intestines hanging out, his partners turned on him, pulled down the two trees, fastened him to them, covered his dangling intestines first in pitch, then in fire, and sent him sailing. He was well lit, and I must confess I found it an amazing sight as his guts strung out long and red and flaming across the dark skyline. A string of the guts caught up in the top of a palm tree at the edge of the shore, lit it on fire, brightening the whole grue-some scene below in an orange-red cast.

Finally, after an hour of drinking and cursing and fighting, the Captain became angry with one of the pirates and slashed the top of the man's head with his cutlass. The blow drove the pirate to the ground, the cutlass hung up in his skull. Balancing on his peg, using his one good foot, the Captain, with a grunt and a shove, pulled his sword free.

Amazingly, the man got up, staggered and fell down. Chunks of his hair, which had been cut by the cutlass blow, fell from his head. The pirates let out a roar of laughter. None louder than the Captain himself. "Good form," he said loud enough for us to hear, and the pirates burst into an even louder peal of laugher.

The pirate who had been struck sat up, put a hand on top of his damaged skull and laughed. Soon, with a wad of bloody cloth stuck to the top of his head, he was laughing and drinking, seemingly no worse for wear.

It was then that I noticed that the great ape had finally stopped turning the wheel, and was leaning against it, looking out at the drunken pirates. The look on his simian face was inscrutable.

I looked at Cat and Bull. Cat was snuggled up close to Bull. And Bull, with one arm around her, looked out at the pirates. His face revealed nothing.

As Mr. Twain had suspected, it wasn't long before the pirates lay all over the beach, passed out. The only people awake were those tied alongside the ship. And, of course, the great red ape.

Mr. Verne pulled the cruiser into shape, and we mounted up, glid-ed down from our hiding place, me at the controls, Mr. Verne holding the pistol. Mr. Twain had the machete, and Passepartout held his club.

It suddenly occurred to me that as much as I had wanted to fight, we were not the most apt group. Neither Verne nor Twain were young men, and Passepartout, though younger than they, did not appear to me to be the fighting type. And I, alas, was a seal.

The firelight from the blazing palm gave the shore an unearthly look, as if we were floating along a corridor of hell. The cruiser was quiet, and not one pirate stirred. The prisoners saw us coming but remained quiet. It occurred to me we might slip in, free them, and escape without ever being heard.

We arrived in front of the prisoners, and with me staying at the controls, the others dismounted. Mr. Twain used the machete to cut the rope, and then to free individual bonds.

When I was on the beach, Bull and Cat saw me. Cat almost cried out, but stifled it by placing a hand to her mouth. I could see her smile at the edge of her hand, the firelight in her eyes. Bull looked up and made with a soft grunt. For Bull, that was pretty excited.

After Mr. Twain cut the prisoners free, I counted them. Including Bull and Cat, there were ten.

One of the men, an official looking fellow in what might have been a blue military jacket and very worn blue pants, came over to us. The other Indian came with him.

The man spoke softly, said, "My name is Bill Beadle, and this is my friend, John Feather. We are glad to see you, as you can imagine."

Twain said, "Thing for us to do is to get out of here quick."

"That's why I'm talking to you," Beadle said. "The ape. He can assist us."

"He can?" Twain said.

"He is not like other apes. But there is no time to explain that. If we free him, he can drag the ship into the water, out deep, and we can sail away on the night tide. The wind is up, and we should be able to make good time. This man," Beadle pointed at a tall lean fellow wearing a dirty cap and soiled whites, "is the Captain. He's called the Dutchman."

The Dutchman nodded.

"But the ape," Mr. Twain said. "Why would he help us, without whips I mean?"

"Trust me for now," Beadle said.

Bull said, "Borrow knife."

Without getting an answer, Bull took Twain's machete, and stalked toward the sleeping pirates.

Twain called to him as softly as possible, but Bull wasn't listening.

Faster than you could say let's scalp somebody, Bull began to systematically cut the throats of sleeping pirates.

All I can say is we were stunned. We stood there amazed as he went quickly and quietly from one to the other, and soon the ground was littered with gurgling, thrashing pirates, clutching at their oozing throats.

He must have cut the throats of seven or eight before any sort of alarm was aroused, and by this time, he had picked up one of the old style rifles from the ground, and had stuffed two cap and ball pistols and the machete into his belt.

He immediately went to work with the firearms.

Bull lifted the rifle and shot one of the pirates full in the face, from less than twenty feet away. There is no need for me to describe the gruesome results, other than to say the fellow, not a pretty sight to began with, went from grimacing and growling and drawing a sabre to suddenly looking as if a cherry pie had exploded in his face.

Bull tossed the one shot weapon aside, drew the pistols, and as bullets rained around him, shot first one man in the temple, by walking right up to him (and keep in mind, this man was firing away and seemed to be in a position impossible to miss Bull, but did) and when this man fell from Bull's shot, another who was armed with a sword decided to make a run for it. Bull gave him a warning shot. Right in the back of the head.

Now we were all scrambling for a hiding place. The bullets were storming about us like windblown hail. Twain darted for the opposite side of the ship, and I followed with the cruiser, but what we found there were more pirates, staggering up from their inebriated slumber.

Mr. Verne, who had come around on that side with us, went to work with the pistol, fired five shots in rapid succession, popping off three pirates, sending the other two shots somewhere out into the ocean, or perhaps smacking into a palm tree. He jerked the box of shells out of his pocket and began reloading. While he was about this task, a pirate with a sword charged down on him. Mr. Twain leaped forward, and luckily slid up under the attacker's arm before the sabre could come down on Mr. Verne, caught the pirate's wrist, and began to wrestle with him. I scooted around behind the pirate on the cruiser, and knocked him down.

Mr. Twain stepped on his hand, liberated him of his sword, and stuck him with it through the throat.

"The ape. Come now."

It was Beadle. He had picked up a piece of driftwood, and I could see that it was covered in blood and brains. Mr. Twain leaped onto the cruiser, as did Beadle, who said, "Fine device," and we flitted over to where the ape was chained to the wheel.

All around us pirates were yelling and attacking, but those Bull had killed provided weapons for our group, and considering what they had seen the pirates do, the folks from the trotline attacked with a fury generally reserved for sharks, who I hate, but I believe I have mentioned that.

I saw Cat leap on a pirate, take him down, and with her teeth she tore at his throat. A spray of blood leaped high and wide and splattered her, coating her black hair with gore. But she was already up, springing onto the back of another pirate.

Down the beach a bit, I saw Beadle's Indian friend on top of a pirate, pounding him in the head with what may have been a coconut.

The air stank of blood and shit, and just the faintest hint of salt spray and fish from the ocean. Believe it or not, the smell of fish made me hungry.

A bullet tore past Mr. Twain's shoulder and grazed my nose. It made me mad. I wished I could have a pistol, because with my flipper backing it, using my thumb, I knew I could fire it. But I had what I had. My head and my ass, and so far, pretty good luck.

⟝⬦⟞

When we reached the ape and the wheel, Passepartout was already there. He had secured a sabre from one of the pirates, and was chopping away at the wheel where it connected to the chains on the ape's wrists.

"Good man," Beadle said.

"I can't stand to see such as this," Passepartout said. "Even if he chooses to kill me, I must set him free."

The ape was very close to Passepartout, and watched the Frenchman at work in a way that could only be described as grateful; unlike most apes, his face was full of human expression. In fact, on close examination, he seemed less ape-like than he had appeared from a distance.

There was something different about the shape of his head, the very human eyes (which, later, in better light I saw to be green), the thin lips and the full ears with lobes. He stood more upright, and unlike apes, who have small penises, this guy had a goober that looked like a four foot switch handle hammer, testicles like grapefruits.

I want to add here that I couldn't help but notice. I mean, it was hanging out there for all to see. It's not that I go around checking out other peoples' or creatures' equipment, but this couldn't help but be noticed. Really. It was big. No shit.

By the time we arrived, Passepartout had chopped away enough of the wheel that the great ape could tug with the chains and cause the wheel to creak and snap, allowing him to pull his hands (paws?) free of it. The chains still dangled from his wrists, and chunks of the wheel dangled from the chains.

While we floated about, keeping a kind of guard, Passepartout went to work on the lower part of the wheel where chains were fastened to the ape's ankles. In short time, he had made swift work of the wood, allowing the ape to jerk those chains free as well.

The ape turned toward the remaining pirates. The chains that were on his ankles were also hooked together, so he could not move swiftly, but he could move quickly enough, in a hopping fashion.

As he hopped, he swung the great chains fastened to his wrists, the chunks of wood fastened to them. He swung them and struck pirates and knocked them about. Shots were fired at the ape, and no doubt at least a couple of them hit him, but it didn't slow him down. He hopped and swung and shattered flesh and bone like a mad wife smashing dinner plates.

I looked up and saw that the pirate captain was hustling up the hill and making good time in spite of his peg leg. I made a barking noise, pointed with my flipper. Mr. Twain saw the Captain's back just before he was enveloped by the lush greenery at the top of the hill.

"It can't be helped," Mr. Twain said, stepping down from the cruiser. "It doesn't matter now. Our business here, bloody as it is, is through. It's not what I had in mind, but after Sitting Bull got the ball rolling, there wasn't much choice."

About that time the gentleman of mention appeared, blood splattered, a fistful of scalps dangling from his left fist, the machete in his right hand. Cat trotted alongside him, her beautiful gore-stained black hair wadded up around her head.

Bull gave the blood-covered machete to Mr. Twain, said, "Thank you."

"You're welcome," Mr. Twain said, tossing aside the pirate sabre to take the machete. "I suppose."

"Little dull. But cut fuckers good."

"I'll have it sharpened."

"Bull do it. Get done right."

"Thanks. I'll let you."

Mr. Verne arrived. "It looks as if we have won," he said. "We have killed most of them, and the others have darted into the woods. Who would have thought it?"

"I think Mr. Bull killed about a third of them himself," Mr. Twain said.

"Kill more," Bull said, "but tired. Hungry. Got anything to eat?"

"I'm afraid not," Mr. Verne said. "But perhaps now we can find something."

The ape appeared. The chains made his movements jerky, but he looked happy. The ape said, "Now, that is exactly what I've been waiting for. The precise moment to take my vengeance on these low grade sea urchins, these coconut heads of the ocean. And I must tell you, I enjoyed every bloodthirsty moment of it. I am invigorated. After being so tired at the wheel, I thought I might drop down and die. Now, I feel as if I could beat the living shit out of twenty more, fuck a hole in a watermelon, and give head to a pack of monkeys."

Our group sat in silence. Me, because I had to, Bull because he preferred to, and Cat because she thought the incident funny. I could tell the remainder of the crowd was shocked that an ape might speak, and that in so doing would have such strange and vulgar language at his command.

I, being a seal who could write and think like a human, and who had experienced many an adventure with beasts who had been transformed into men or women (Cat was an example) and who could talk, was less impressed.

"You would do that?" Mr. Verne asked the ape.

"Do what?"

"You know? With monkeys."

"It's an expression," the ape said."I really don't have a thing for monkeys. Or watermelons."

"Damn," Mr. Twain said. "A talking monkey."

"I am neither monkey nor ape," corrected the red furred creature. "And the name is Rikwalk."

"That's quite a name," Beadle said.

"Well, it's really very common where I come from."

"And, if I might inquire," Mr. Verne said. "Where is that?"

"Mars," said the ape.

We all stood on the beach considering that. I thought I was beyond surprise, but this did surprise me. We remained hushed and still, listening as it were to the crash of the sea on the shore, the cry of the birds, and the loud thudding silence of death.

Sixteen

Ned's Journal: The Ship Sails Again, the Thing in the Hold, Rikwalk Gets Pants

"**D**id you come with the Invaders?" Mr. Verne asked.

"Not exactly," Rikwalk said, "but it is a long story."

"I suggest we wait on it," said John, "push the ship to sea. Lest our escaped pirates return, possibly with reinforcements."

"I doubt he had any," Beadle said.

"Still, I have had all of this island I prefer," said John Feather.

"Speak good white man talk," Bull said. "Like me."

"Thank you," John Feather said. "College."

"And like our friend Rikwalk here, I presume you have quite a story yourself," Mr. Verne said, smiling at John Feather.

"Oh," said John Feather laughing. "You can not imagine. But like Rikwalk's story, Beadle and I will save it for later."

Rikwalk said, "I will pull the ship to sea, and then it is up to the Dutchman here to sail it."

"I can do that," said the Dutchman. "The remainder of my crew will help me, and they will train the rest of you where your assistance is needed. But that will be minimal. It takes few to sail my ship."

"Work for me," Bull said.

———❖———

Using tools from the ship, Rikwalk was released from the chains, and we all loaded onto the ship, taking what weapons we could scrounge from the remains of the pirates.

The great ape, using the chain attached to the front of the ship, pulled us out to sea.

He had a bit of tough sledding at first, but when he reached the water, and the ship glided in behind him, it went well. He waded until the water was beneath his armpits and we were enough at sea to let the waves carry us out, then he swam back to the ship, scuttled up over the side like, well, like an ape. His weight was such that this maneuver caused the ship to list to that side.

Once on board, however, the ship balanced out nicely. A breeze came up, the sails were hoisted. The wind caught in the canvas and took us out quickly.

When I looked back, I saw, sailing above the jungle, a strange colorful creature that looked more reptile than bird, and yet, somewhat bird-like as well. It was our old friend the pterodactyl, or one just like him.

The cruiser had been put up, and I was raised up on my ass, leaning against the rail. I reached over and tugged on Mr. Twain's coat.

He turned for a look, said, "I'll be goddamned."

Mr. Verne and the others looked now.

Bull said. "Firebird. Me hear of it."

The pterodactyl descended into the mist that covered the island, and was gone.

"I would like to know what other beasts dwell there," Mr. Verne said.

"I'm glad we left," said John Feather. "The pirates were beast enough for me."

"I wonder where they came from," Mr. Verne said. "They looked, well, out of time. In fact, this ship, this crew, looks out of time as well."

"They are," Beadle said. "But again, I'll explain what I know later. Each for different reasons. For now, I suggest we get well out to sea, rest a bit, see if the Dutchman has some food, and afterward we can talk."

"Yee haw," Bull said out of nowhere.

———◆———

Most of the sailing was left to those who knew how to sail. In the battle with the pirates, not a man from the ship had been lost, and each of them knew their business. They scuttled from rope to canvas, and the Dutchman, tall and noble looking, stood at the wheel. If he didn't know what he was doing, he sure looked as if he knew.

We helped where we could, but after a point, we were more trouble than we were worth. That being the case, a number of us naturally drifted together. Mr. Twain, Mr. Verne, myself, Mr. Beadle, John Feather, Bull, and Cat, and the great ape Rikwalk.

Mr. Beadle determined that we all (I dismiss myself from this group) might be a smidgen more comfortable, as he put it, if we could talk Rikwalk into wearing something over his sizeable member.

It is my belief that this had less to do with modesty than with embarrassment. Comparatively, human penises are worms while Rikwalk's member was an anaconda. I read about them in books. They are big snakes, by the way. Real big snakes.

I, who am not particularly endowed, do not go about with my tool poking out except when I mean business, as you might surmise. And I do not wear clothes, unless, for some reason, I feel sporty. I do like my fez, though. I thought it made me look like a seal with an attitude.

However, I must admit, in all honesty, when I was not mentioned as someone who should wear something over myself, I had a flash of insecurity. A sort of, hey, if you want him clothed, what about me? I'm naked as the proverbial jaybird here and no one's concerned.

But I let that go. I reached down inside myself and found that reservoir of strength I knew I had, and pulled it up tight, secure in my manhood and in the necessary size of my equipment.

After all, I am but a little seal, so what should one expect?
Right?
Rikwalk is a giant. Proportionately, there is no real difference.
Well, maybe a little.
Perhaps more than a little.
Still, it's the not the meat, it's the motion.
Right?
That's right, isn't it?
I believe that's right.
I really do.

Anyway, the matter was broached, and Rikwalk took it well. In fact, he seemed to like the idea. Some sailcloth was found, and some rope, and Rikwalk was appropriately tricked out in a large diaper-style adornment. Cat said she didn't see it as an improvement. Bull thought this was very funny.

When Rikwalk was attired, Mr. Beadle said that he had something interesting he wanted to show us in the hold, and that there was a story to go with it, but he thought it might be interesting to have Rikwalk tell us his story first, and upon its completion, he would take us into the interior of the ship, show us what he wished to have us view, then tell us a tale about himself and John Feather.

This all seemed rather exciting, (less exciting than our previous experiences, but a sort of excitement you could look forward to) and so we gathered ourselves on the deck near the mainsail, the moon low down and bright, the sail above us beating in the wind like a hummingbird's wings, a cool salt spray blowing across the deck, and we sat, and Rikwalk talked.

Ned's Journal Ends

Part Three:

Heroes Unite

Seventeen

Rikwalk's Story, Beadle's Tale, the Thing in the Hold

Once upon a time, on Rikwalk's world, in Rikwalk's universe, at a specific angle of dimensional division, this happened:

On one of many planets called Mars, where the universe splits sideways and turns cattycorner and anglewise, there was a rip in the sky and things fell out of it.

There were other rips, and into these rips, things fell up, and out of some of the rips, more things fell down.

Ups and downs. Rips this way and that.

Besides the rips, the ups and downs, what was happening was that, like a hand slowly balling up a sheet of paper, the fabrics of times and spaces were being wadded one into the other, and all of existence was soon to be no more than a tight wad of all things known and things unknown. The Wild West, Flying Saucers, Rock and Roll, Super Heroes, all manner of times, yesterdays and tomorrows, real lives and imagined lives, and as the wad grew tighter, these worlds, these things, would cease to exist.

It wasn't a pretty picture, and this is how Rikwalk discovered there was a picture, and that things were coming together and coming apart.

———◆———

So Rikwalk is living on Mars, you see, and not the Mars that Twain and Verne look up and see. Not the Mars from which the invaders came to ravage the world of Twain and Verne, but another Mars. Not the Mars that is worn out and sandy, near airless and waterless, but a lush Mars, ripe as a nubile virgin in stretch pants. A Mars crisscrossed by canals and greenery and strange animals and shining cities in which lived what to our eyes would appear to be sophisticated giant apes with big dongs.

But there are other Marses. Some with apes. Some without. Some with the invaders. And some without anything but hot, red soil.

These Marses, these universes, these dimensions, it's like there's a train on a track, and under the track is another train, and they're alike and run the same way, but inside the train, people do different things. Sometimes the same people, or apes, or insects, or creatures, but these beings are multiplied, taking different paths, unaware of their counterparts, or their differparts. And say alongside the train, if you could slice into its metal skin, slice it real thin, you would find there's another train in there, running parallel with the first train. Each train (each universe) and its contents (think humanity, apeanity, insectimanity, etc.) believes it is the Union Pacific and no other Union Pacifics exist. But if you could hold a special mirror to the top of the train, you would see that, in fact, there's a train on its back, its smokestack meeting the stack of the other, and its wheels turning on a track that is touching ground that should be sky in the other universe.

And don't forget that train on the bottom of the track. Don't forget that. And on the sides, under the skins. Don't forget them. And, understand, that from all these trains are other trains, atop, abottom, and asides.

It's all in the angles, baby. And, from one train's angle, the other angle does not exist, and yet, all angles exist.

Omniscient narrator is getting a headache, baby, so he's gonna back off and say this:

Say on one train operations are as smooth as married sex, but on the other, well, it's more like adolescent boys trying to determine which hole what goes in. And on some trains, they can't even get their pants down, or haven't figured out they ought to wear pants.

Say there's a warp in the track. A bad warp. Call it trouble with the universe. Maybe a black hole caused it. Something we don't understand yet. Time(s) and Space(s), for whatever reason, begin(s) to collapse on itself.

So this train, running on this track, hits the warped stretch and bumps up into the train below. Or maybe the warp throws the train off the tracks, and the train on the bottom, and the one on the top, and the ones on the sides, all come together. Now, finally, they are aware of the other. And it's not a happy awareness.

———◆———

Rikwalk's Martians called themselves the Mellie and they called their planet Mars.

And so Rikwalk, he's living on his Mars, and things are good. He's got a job operating one of the locks on one of the canals, and it's a good job. He's making good pay, doesn't work hard, gets a little over-time, has a wife he loves, one of the good ones that hasn't stopped giving head after ten years of marriage, and he's got a daughter and a son, two groodies and a zup.(3) And one day he's out at the lock, ready to check the water depth with a dropping gauge, and he hears something that sounds like a runner's tendon ripping from too much tension, looks up, sees a fiery orange-red rip in the sky. At first, he thinks he sees the sun, but it isn't. Not even close. It's a glowing rip to nowhere.

A boat in the lock is suddenly sucked up and through the rip, falls out of sight into orange-redness. The rip widens, and Rikwalk is sucked up, like a dust mote in a vacuum cleaner. Sucked right up toward the glowing rip in the sky.

Rikwalk goes through it, comes down in a place he doesn't know. The boat isn't there, and he doesn't know where in hell it went. Another exit?

Actually, he comes out, not down. Because in spite of going up, coming through the rift, the exit is to the side, sort of, and it has this ripple effect going. Like a heat wave.

Rikwalk falls out, hits the ground, the orange-red rip closes up like a tear in a persimmon pushed together by a cheating fruit salesman.

Now there is just this thin as razor edge, orange-red line in the air, and when Rikwalk reaches out to touch it, hoping to go back through,

---

3. Martian farm animals on Rikwalk's Mars. One gives milk, the other gives eggs. That's all you need to know.

to take his chances, try and fall down into the waters of his lock, the line vibrates and tightens like an old maid who's considered the deed then changed her mind.

No more split.

No more glow.

Not even a line, man.

———✦———

"So you see," said Rikwalk, "the rips came and went at first, and then some of them started staying. You could see holes in the sky, and sudden rips in the air right before you. All sorts of people and things came out of them. Some of the stuff I saw made the hair on my ass stand up.

"I decided to look about at first, and for a moment, I thought I was still on my world. But it was a horrible world of the living dead. They walked about. They attacked people."

"Living Dead?" Verne said. "What do you mean?"

"Mellie? Apes to you. The dead were rising from their graves and they were trying to kill the living, eat their flesh."

Ned wrote: WOW. FLESH-EATING APES WITH BIG DICKS THAT SPEAK ENGLISH.

"The dead," Rikwalk said, "they are not sweet to smell. And there's no reason I can offer to explain their rising. You died there, you came back. A virus maybe. Caused by the splits in space and time, perhaps. I don't know. But let me address this matter of speaking English. On my world, this language you call English is Mellie. I have no explanation for it being the same language. A few words, expressions are different. But it's mostly the same. Why? Shit, I don't know. It just is. But from a few books I've seen here on board ship—and I'll explain my being on the ship earlier as I come to it—we have a better approach to spelling."

"I think we all get the idea," Beadle said. "Sort of. Just go on with your story."

Rikwalk nodded. Said: "So there I am. Pursued by the living dead, shuffling along, their hands held out, the hair on their faces falling off, their tongues thick and black. And I'm running like a bastard. They're after my ass. Want to eat me. Or kill me and turn me like them. If they don't eat all of you, you get up and you're hungry. And we're not talking wanting a slice of doonbar loaf and two pieces of bread."

"What's a doonbar?" Mr. Twain said. "Is that English?"

"Sorry," Rikwalk said. "That's one of the different words. It's kind of like a turkey. Only not."

"Close enough," Mr. Twain said. "Go on."

"They want Mellie flesh. No cooking. No seasoning. On the hoof, fresh and hot. And when you turn, when you're like them, even if your legs are cut off, you'll crawl after your prey."

"Was everyone on that world dead?" Twain asked.

"No. There were plenty dealing with the problem, same as me. Let me tell you something interesting. After a short time, people went back to work. Like always. They just carried weapons. You see, you could kill them if you burned them or cut off their heads. So people carried big knives. Thing about the dead, they're not very strong and they're not very fast, and smart isn't even a minor factor in the equation. On a smart scale of one to ten, they're not on it... Yes, Ned?"

Ned held up his pad.

THAT'S SCARY.

"Yes, it is, Ned," Rikwalk said. "It's even scarier when they're chasing you."

"But that doesn't explain how you're here," Twain said.

"No. It doesn't. So I'm on this world that isn't my world, but it's similar, and I'm doing the best I can to survive, and the sky, it starts to be marked all over with rips, like lesions. And finally, one day, sick of it all, sick of dodging and fighting, I stepped into one of the rips."

"That shows you have some real plums," Twain said.

"Or that I'm stupid. I could have fallen anywhere. Up, down, sideways. Actually, I did end up anywhere. I stepped through a slit in time, and fortunately, did not fall, just stepped sideways, ended up in Beadle's world."

"Couldn't the dead follow?" Verne asked.

"They did. They followed me in. A few of them. I dispatched them. The wound in the sky closed. True, another wound would open somewhere else, but there was no telling where it would lead. Back to the dead world. My world. Your world. Any world. Shortly thereafter, I met Beadle, John Feather, and Steam."

"Steam?" Passepartout said.

"Perhaps it's best if I let Mr. Beadle take over the story," Rikwalk said. "Then I'll finish, and then we'll all finish with a look in the hold."

"The Dark Rider," Beadle said. "He was the problem."

"With what?" Twain asked. "What kind of problem?"

WHO THE FUCK IS THE DARK RIDER?

"Bad language, little seal," Mr. Verne said.

I'M SORRY. BUT WHO THE FUCK IS THE DARK RIDER?

"The rips in the sky, tears in the universe," John Feather. "You name it, Dark Rider was behind it all. If he wasn't sticking his dick in someone's asshole, he was poking it through time, waving it in space."

"Interesting expressions," Verne said. "Very American sounding. You are American?"

"Where I come from, we are Americans. But I have no idea if the America here is the same."

"Well, you speak American," Twain said. "I should know. I'm American. You cuss like an American. Only Americans truly know how to cuss. Cussing is an art, and not to be used without intent and discrimination. My wife cussed, but bless her soul, so poorly it was hardly worth hearing. It requires true training and timing to cuss properly."

"You and Verne exist in our world," Beadle said. "I thought I should mention that."

"Really?" Twain said.

"Yes. You write books."

"Same alike here," Twain said. "But I must apologize. You were talking about this Dark Rider fella."

"We don't know much about him. But not long ago, we went back to where we battled him. Went back after we recovered and repaired Steam, and we found his diary. You see, we defeated him. It's a long story and I don't want go into it, but we did. We left the scene of the battle, recovered, went back and found the diary."

"Again," Twain said, "sorry to interrupt, but who is Steam?"

"I'm coming to that," Beadle said. "As I said, I won't tell you the whole of mine and John's story. (4) But I'll tell you some. I'll give you some background. I'll link to Rikwalk's tale. The world Rikwalk came into was as chaotic as the world of the dead. Maybe more so. On our world, time and space were ripping and collapsing at an alarming rate. Maybe it's like that on a lot of other worlds, but this one, strange as it is to me, is nothing like what our world became. There are fewer rips. Less collapsing.

"Me and John Feather were part of an organization. I formed it. There was me and John, two others. You need not know them, know all the past. But we were trying to set wrongs right. When our world started coming apart, all manner of things came through the rips, and we decided to use our man of steam to correct them."

"A steam man," Twain said. "We have dime novels about such things. Steam horses. Steam this and steam that. Jules here, who is far better than a dime novelist, has written about such. I have been in such a machine. A boat designed by Jules, built by Passepartout. It ran at extraordinary speeds. It also came apart."

Ned wrote furiously. THERE IS NOTHING WRONG WITH DIME NOVELS. I LIKE DIME NOVELS. I SELDOM THINK OF FISH WHEN I'M READING A DIME NOVEL. WHEN I READ FLAUBERT, I THINK OF FISH A LOT. I LIKE MR. TWAIN'S AND MR. VERNE'S NOVELS. I DON'T THINK ABOUT FISH WHEN I READ THEM.

"Point taken," Twain said. "And thanks for the compliment."

"Yes, Ned," Verne said. "Thank you."

"Sorry, Beadle," Twain said. "Done it again. Please go ahead. You were saying about correcting the bad things on your world with the use of the steam man."

Beadle nodded.

---

4. Beadle's world and his and John Feather's adventures and greater background for his story are provided in the dime novel, *The Steam Man of the Prairie and the Dark Rider Get Down* by Joe R. Lansdale. Another version of this story, based on Ned The Seal's translation of a more detailed story told to him later by Beadle is available in some rare book collections as *The Steam Man of the Prairie and the Incredible Vampire Traveler From Beyond*. The Lansdale version is more readily available.

"Steam was a big metal man. He didn't have brains. Didn't have a heart. Didn't have courage. He was a machine. Built forty feet tall, not counting his conical hat. He was twenty feet wide and tin-colored. Powered by steam. Puffed steam when he walked. He was strong. He could tear trees up by the roots, toss big boulders, wade furious streams. You see, we were his heart, brains and courage, me and John Feather, our two friends. It saddens me so much to think of them I can hardly speak of it. It was the Dark Rider who killed them."

"The Dark Rider was our nemesis," John Feather said.

Beadle nodded. "I believe he is responsible for the rifts in our world, and for that matter, all the worlds. Time travel was not meant to be. It makes holes in the fabric of time, makes it look like Swiss cheese."

Ned wrote: THAT'S CHEESE WITH HOLES IN IT. I LIKE CHEESE. NOT AS MUCH AS FISH, BUT IT GOES WELL WITH FISH. DO YOU HAVE ANY CHEESE OR FISH? I ENJOY A STORY BEST ON A FULL STOMACH. I HAVE EVEN BEEN KNOWN TO EAT OLIVES.

Everyone present admitted they had neither fish nor cheese nor olives.

VERY WELL. BUT, IF YOU THINK OF ANYTHING YOU MIGHT HAVE THAT A SEAL WOULD EAT, AND IN MY CASE THAT'S QUITE VARIED, PLEASE SPEAK UP. REALLY.

Beadle went on with his story.

"We fought this horrible man who traveled through time, and we defeated him. Forcing him through a rip in time, where we hope he will forever be trapped. When it was over, we got out of there. Meaning the place where we had been tortured and the both of us nearly died, this place where the Time Traveler had been holed up with a group of monster men called Morlocks. We went away from there and licked our wounds and repaired Steam, and when me and John were strong again, we went back.

"The Time Traveler was dead, or lost, out of the way, and we had suffered great indignities at his hands, and at the hands of his Morlocks, but still, we went back."

"Couldn't help ourselves," John Feather said.

"Couldn't," Beadle said. "We went back to maybe see if he had somehow survived. But the rip, it was closed up, and there was no sign of him. But in the rubble of what had been his hideout—"

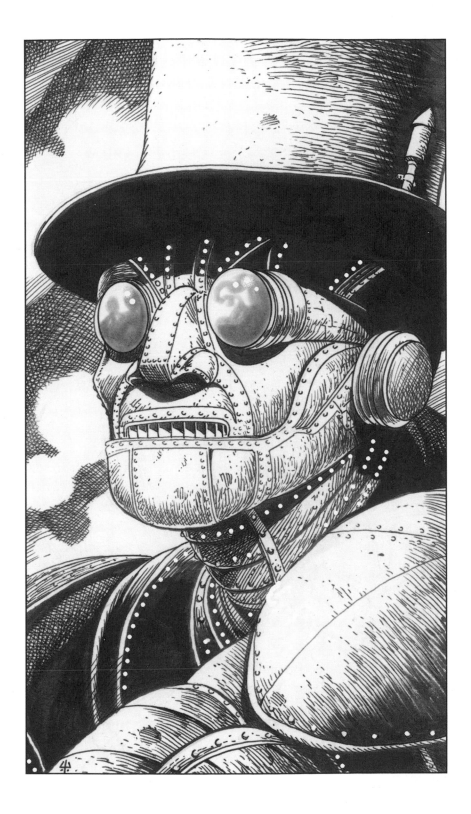

"—it was rubble because Steam destroyed it," John Feather said. "With me at the controls."

"Yee haw," Bull said.

"That's right," Beadle said. "Yee haw. We found what was left of the time machine in the rubble, and we dug it out and pulverized it. We found the diary.

"From the way it read, he had once been whole. His mind good, but the time travel, the things that happened to him, they changed him."

"He turned evil as an old boll weevil," John Feather said.

"That's right," Beadle said. "And all that time traveling, bringing the Morlocks through time, it punched holes in the fabric of things. Anyway, there we were, with the diary, looking through the rubble, and we decided to leave, and the world tore open."

"The bottom fell out," John Feather said.

"And we dropped through," Beadle said. "Splashed in the ocean. But we were lucky. We were near the shore and Steam landed on his feet. The water was up to his neck, but his feet were on the bottom. The water didn't get in. He was built airtight and we had done a lot of repairs. The fire didn't go out. We were able to walk him toward shore."

"This is where I must butt in," Rikwalk said. "Somehow, I came through the same rip with them. Or right behind them. I was on their world already, and I remember seeing the man of steam from a distance. I didn't want to get close, not knowing them. And I saw them go through the rift, and I thought, shit, bad luck for them. And then the rip widened. And I started to run, but it widened faster than I could run, so I was sucked in too. I fell in the ocean, swam toward shore. I saw the steam man ahead of me. Beadle and John Feather were inside Steam, though, of course I did not know that, nor did I know them at the time. Steam was walking onto the shore, moving toward the curtain of mist. That catches my story up for now. Please, Mr. Beadle, Mr. Feather. Continue."

"But then luck turned on us," John Feather said.

"Seems to be the story of our lives," Beadle said. "Turning luck, mostly turning for the bad. There were pirates on the shore. You know the boys. You've met them. They quickly surrounded Steam, and using ropes, they were able to take him down. You see, we had used what steam he had left to fight the current and make shore. He just didn't have the strength. And they got Rikwalk."

"They saw me swimming," Rikwalk said, "and it was a battle, that current, and when I came onto the shore I was so weak I couldn't stand. I crawled, gasping for air. They pounced on me like fleas. If I had had my full strength, I would have killed them all. But like Steam, I had used all my reserves. They chained me. They fastened me to the wheel. And then they whipped me. I really didn't have a choice but to help them."

"We were all in a weak condition," Beadle said. "And for the most part, John and I were already weakened. Our battle with the Dark Rider. The torture. Our world coming apart. We were quite the mess. Then Steam playing out. We were at the pirates' mercy."

"I suppose the pirates arrived out of time and space from some other place, through a rip in time," Mr. Verne said.

Beadle nodded. "So I believe. They made slaves of us for a week. They had us bury gold, they made us help them make their grog. My guess is after they had enough barrels of grog for their ship, we would have been disposed of. Lucky for us, they drank what we made as fast as we made it."

"That was lucky," John Feather said.

"What about the Dutchman?" Passepartout said.

"He came the next day. The pirates spotted the ship, and took it over. Some of the Dutchman's men were killed. The ship was grounded on the reef. It wasn't until today that the pirates worked it off, beached it, and then had Rikwalk drag it ashore."

HOW DID BULL AND CAT GET ON THE SHIP. I THOUGHT YOU WERE EATEN BY SHARKS WHEN THE *NAUGHTY LASS* BLEW UP.(5) I DO NOT LIKE SHARKS.

Ned turned his sign toward Bull. Bull, though he seldom gave sign of it, could read basic English well. He said:

"Not eaten. *Naughty Lass* sink. Real shit time. Go down faster than white whore in buffalo camp. We get away. Boat pick up. Kill two pirates before get hit in head. Get even with their asses."

"I'll say," Twain said.

---

5. *Zeppelins West*

The Dutchman suddenly appeared. A sailor had taken his place at the wheel. "I couldn't help but overhear," the Dutchman said. "I believe that I fit into the story about here. When we saw the pirates, knew we could not outrun them, and that we would be engaged, we pushed Cat's hair under a big hat. I gave her a large shirt to pull over the one she wore, to hide her attributes. When we were ashore, we stayed as close to her as we could manage, trying not to allow too much scrutiny of her body. But you can only hide a figure like that for so long. I think the pirates were starting to think she might be a boy they could learn to love, and then, as fate would have it, the wind blew her hat off. They pulled up the long shirt, looked at her rear, looked down her pants. I'm surprised she was not raped."

"Actually," Beadle said, "the pirate captain saved her. He didn't give a reason, but he had the men leave her alone. I believe he thought to have her for himself later on."

"Now he has an island full of monsters to call his very own," Verne said.

"What happened to Steam?" Twain said.

"They robbed what they could find inside Steam," Beadle said. "They stuck him in the hold of the Dutchman's ship. I don't know why. Maybe they thought to dismantle him. Sell off the metal. Melt it down. I don't know. It took all of the pirates and us as well to drag him over the side, and push him down into the hold. They weren't easy with him, and he may be damaged down there."

"So that's what you wanted us to see in the hold?" Twain said.

"Yes," Beadle said.

Twain and Verne, taking turns, with the occasional comment from Passepartout and sign writing from Ned, told their story, about the Martian invaders, how they had come to the island.

Rikwalk said, "I would like to, on behalf of the Mars from whence I come, apologize for these other Martians. They give us a bad name."

"Apology accepted," Twain said. "But I'm still curious about why you speak English."

"I'm afraid I can't shed light on that," Rikwalk said. "I have ideas, but nothing concrete."

"Shall we take that look in the hold now?" Beadle said. "I'm curious to see how Steam weathered his drop down the chute."

"I'll conduct that tour," the Dutchman said. "After all, it is my ship."

—⸱⸱⸱—

They followed the Dutchman to a pair of closed doors positioned and bolted shut in the floor of the deck. Beadle unbolted and opened them. There were stairs. They went down with the Dutchman in the lead.

The Dutchman lit a lantern hanging on a peg, and in the middle of the hold's floor they saw an amazing sight.

A giant metal man with a conical hat, like a funnel turned upside down.

"Steam," Beadle said. "If not in the flesh. In the metal."

And so it was.

Big.

Tall.

Silver.

Stained glass windows for eyes.

Steam.

Eighteen

At Sea, the White Cliffs of Dover, the Invaders Seen from Afar

The morning arrived clear and crisp. The sea was calm and the wind was smooth. The sailing ship moved swiftly. Flying fish glided, porpoises leaped. A cool wind was not only in the sails, it was in the faces of its crew and passengers.

Ned, his nose hanging over the rail, wet with spray, full of the smell of salt, was in heaven.

Twain, Verne, Ned, Passepartout, John Feather, and Beadle had joined the Dutchman, the ship's captain, on the foredeck. They stood there while the Dutchman maintained the wheel, observed sky, sea, and sails.

Rikwalk was seated down below, but his head almost reached the wheel deck. His red fur was crusted in places with salt. And in the bright morning light, wounds could be seen. Someone, the Dutchman perhaps, had treated them with black grease to keep out infection and dirt.

While they talked, Twain and the Dutchman smoked long black cigars.

Twain said, "Does anyone know where we are? I suppose we are not sailing at random."

"The Island of Mist, as the pirates called it," the Dutchman said, "was off the southwest coast of Africa. So, we are moving north along the coast of Africa."

"My God," Twain said. "The balloon sailed that far?"

"It must have," the Dutchman said, "because that's where you were. And along the coast of Africa is where you are now."

"How amazing," Verne said. "And even more amazing, I saw an actual flying dinosaur."

"So it seems," the Dutchman said. "It is said, that in the depths of the Congo there are dinosaurs, and even an ape near the size of our hairy red friend. I do not know that it is true, but it is said. And if there are such things on the Island of Mist, I suppose it's possible."

"And where do you sail?" Rikwalk asked.

"I am at your disposal. As for me, it matters not where I sail. I am to suffer ill fate. Storms and pirates. But I never die and the ship never sinks. And I always end up back at sea. No matter how often I dock, fate always leads me back to the ship and to the open sea. I am cursed."

"My God," Twain said. "You're not that Dutchman, are you?"

"I am."

"The Flying Dutchman?" Verne said.

"The one and only. That's what the ship is called. It is written in German, my ancestry, on the side of the ship. I am not Dutch at all. But like many Germans, I am lumped under the label."

The term Flying Dutchman didn't register on Rikwalk's radar, so they filled him in. They often had to stop and fill him in. He was, after all, a Martian. An English speaking Martian, but a Martian.

"But I thought you couldn't stop sailing at all," Passepartout said. "Isn't that the legend?"

"There are many legends," the Dutchman said, "but I am not a legend. I am sadly real. I can stop, and because I can, I thought at first there was no curse, that the witch had failed. I was wrong. First time I stopped and went ashore, I was shanghaied, hit in the head and tossed on my own ship, which was stolen. I eventually wrested it from the thieves, but I was wounded horribly. I survived, and I was still at sea. One day the sky opened up in front of me, and me and my crew and I sailed through a rift. It was not a dramatic event. We merely seemed to glide through a red rip in the sky, onto other waters that looked to be the same as the ocean we had been on moments before. I thought it was an optical illusion. Like a mirage. It was just another in a long line of events and disasters. I was in another time and place. This place. Then there were the pirates. I no longer fight my fate. There is no use."

Ned wrote:

THAT'S TOUGH. THAT EATS THE BIG OLD FAT DONKEY DICK BUNCHES.

"You can say that again, Ned," the Dutchman said."I was cursed by a witch because I seduced her daughter. You want to know something? It wasn't worth it. She wasn't that good, and she wasn't that clean. Even pussy isn't worth this."

Twain, Verne, Passepartout, Beadle, and Ned paused to consider this. No one agreed nor disagreed. It was like a Catholic cursing the Madonna. That kind of criticism was not taken lightly. Even in the face of indisputable evidence, men find it hard to turn against pussy, so silence ruled. Ned did not write.

Verne cleared his throat. "So can you sail us to Europe?"

"If that's what you want," the Dutchman said. "But why would you want to if it's covered with those Martian machines?"

"Because we should do something," Verne said. "And because they are bound to be all over the world. My guess is you will face them yourself eventually, and I am warning you, they are formidable."

"Most likely I will face them," The Dutchman said. "And I will struggle against them. And I must ask myself again and again why I even struggle. No matter how it ends, I will be at sail again. I can not die. The ship can be damaged, but never destroyed. I have even tried to kill myself. Tried to cut my own throat. I suffered a horrible wound. It healed. I have been wounded many other times in many different ways. But no matter how violent the wounds, in time they heal, and I live. And I continue."

WHY DON'T YOU JUST SET FIRE TO THE SHIP AND BURN IT UP AND YOU WON'T HAVE TO SAIL IN IT ANYMORE?

The Dutchman was quiet for a time. "I hadn't thought of that Ned...But then again, a wind would probably just blow the fire out...But I could try it."

WHEN WE ARE OFF THE SHIP. RIGHT?

The Dutchman did not answer. He seemed lost in thought.

"You can really just drop us off most anywhere," Twain said.

⟹◈⟸

They sailed on, though they slept nervously for a few nights and sniffed for smoke. Ned did a lot of apologizing, but after a couple days they decided that the Dutchman was not going to set fire to his ship, least not while they were aboard.

They hoped.

Several days more and they could see the English shoreline. The land stood out high and white in the sunlight.

"The White Cliffs of Dover," Verne said.

"Correct," the Dutchman said.

They were at the wheel with the Dutchman again, Verne, Twain, Ned, and Passepartout. Rikwalk lay on the deck, his head cradled on his arm, sleeping. Beadle and John Feather were in the hold, finishing up repairs on Steam. Bull and Cat were below as well. They were below a lot. They were not making repairs on anything. Bull explained it once this way: "Hair pie."

"I decided to bring you here, to these shores," the Dutchman said, "because I thought if the Martian Machines land here, or in America, they have a better chance of being defeated by the English or the Americans than anyone else."

"You are saying the French can not defeat these machines?" Verne said. His and Passepartout's faces scrunched with irritation.

"I am saying, if the Machines want a croissant or a bottle of perfume, France is the place to be. If they want a fight, England or America or Japan is the place to be."

"I take offense to those remarks," Verne said.

"I really don't worry about who I offend or don't," the Dutchman said. "I live forever, unfortunately. I go on and on, and no matter what is done to me, I live. Stab me. Shoot me. I will endure."

"I have no interest in any such solution to an insult," Verne said. "Though I doubt you would endure a shot to the head."

"It was not meant to insult you, Mr. Verne, or you, Passepartout. But I no longer worry about insults. It was a statement of what I believe to be fact. And though I believe in the individual Frenchman's bravery, and you have demonstrated your own, as a country, when it comes to war, you lack a certain something. Perhaps you are too individual."

"That is one way of saying it," Verne said. "But I am not sure I like that better."

SEALS ARE SURPRISINGLY TOUGH, Ned wrote: WE ARE NOT FRENCH.

"I have no comment on the general toughness of seals," the Dutchman said, "but on an individual level, you, my friend, are a tough little seal. And smart as well. I am giving your idea serious consideration. About the fire, I mean."

Ned made a facial expression that might have been a grin.

"I don't even like croissants," Verne said.

"Don't lie," Twain said. "I've seen you eat them."

"I've eaten them, but that doesn't mean I like them. I tasted them. I didn't swallow."

"I like them," Passepartout said. "And I refuse to feel shame for myself. Or the great country of France."

Ned wrote: I AGREE. FRENCHMEN, ENGLISHMEN, AMERICANS. WE ARE ALL THE SAME. EXCEPT ME. I'M DIFFERENT. DO THE FRENCH LIKE FISH?

"Well, yes," Passepartout said.

THE FRENCH ARE A OKAY BY ME...WHAT KIND OF FISH?

"Most any kind," Passepartout said.

ARE YOU SURE YOU ARE NOT A SEAL?

Passepartout laughed, then the others joined in.

Ned, proud of himself, made with the strange seal grin again.

———⊰♦⊱———

They sailed along the English Channel, and from the sea they could see black smoke, and even once, in the distance, what they thought might be one of the great Martian stalking machines.

"I suggest we sail up the channel a bit, find an appropriate place to go ashore," the Dutchman said. "But, if I were you, I would stay with me, take to the sea. Forget the idea of fighting these machines."

"Unlike you," Verne said, "we are willing to take our chances trying to do some good here. And sir, if I may bring it up again, for someone who maligns the French, and for someone who can not die, you seem determined to stay away from the fight."

"I find little purpose in much of anything," the Dutchman said.

"That is sad," Verne said. "Very sad."

"Have it as you wish," the Dutchman said. "You, Mr. Twain, I could let them off here, sail you to America."

"I would like that," Twain said. "But I assume America is dealing with these same machines. If I'm going to try and do something, it might as well be here."

"But what can you do?" the Dutchman said.

"You have been a pessimist too long," Twain said. "I am not alone. I have my friends. Ned, Passepartout and Verne. And new friends as well, Beadle and John Feather, Bull and Cat.

"Bull and Cat not leave ship."

It was Bull. He was coming up the steps that led to the wheel deck. Cat was with him.

"You're staying?" the Dutchman said.

"Me stay. Cat stay. We like ship. Stop get supplies. Go back to sea. Help sail boat."

"The Martians, they will come to sea eventually," Verne said.

"Bad things always come. Always find. Men from rock in sky come, me and Cat fight. But now, we sail. Like life. On land, always cocksucker want trouble. Bull tired of trouble. Like big boat. Help out. Learn chess from Dutchman. Hump Cat. Good life."

"Me-ow," Cat said.

"Well then," Twain said, "we wish you luck, friends."

Bull stuck out his hand and took Twain's. "Bull and Cat wish friends luck. Bull miss Ned much. Ned is brave."

"And sweet," Cat said, giving Ned a kiss on the nose.

The little seal stuck out his chest.

"Much luck," Bull said. "You need it."

⸺⬦⬦⸺

There was a hiss from below, and out of the open hold came a puff of steam followed by a shiny point of silver metal. Then Steam's head, his multi-colored, stained glass eyes appeared.

Steam climbed out of the hold and in a moment was on deck, walking slowly toward them. It was disconcerting. Steam was a great tall man of metal, but there was something about him that made him seem like a living thing. When he walked, his body moved the way a human's does when it walks. It turned its head in an inquisitive manner, like a man looking for a certain street. It was hard to believe there were men at the controls.

Steam stopped, stood still. A trap in his bottom opened up, a ladder poked out, and down it came Beadle and John Feather.

"He works fine," Beadle said as he climbed up on the wheel deck.

"We used some of the wood down there," John Feather said. "I am sorry we did not ask. We actually broke off a few cabinet doors and put them in the furnace. We can only offer our apologies. We should have asked. But then again, we are desperate, sir."

"Apology accepted," the Dutchman said. "But had you asked, and had I said no, would you have done it anyway?"

"I suppose we would have," Beadle said. "We feel that we must. We want to go ashore, help our friends here deal with the Martian Machines. And we want to find our way home. Such as it is."

John Feather said, "We're not so sure we have a home anymore. Our world was in bad shape. But if we could study the diary of the Time Traveler in greater detail, perhaps with the help of scientists, or science minded people, we could figure out what is happening to the universe. If our theory that Time Travel is causing rips in time and space is true, perhaps we could find a cure, so to speak."

"I know people who might help us," Verne said. "A number of them. I am no slouch in scientific matters myself, and Passepartout, my butler, is more than a butler. He is a genius."

"Why, thank you, monsieur," Passepartout said.

"It is only the truth," Verne said. "Passepartout here is the author of many an invention."

"The boat fell apart," Twain said. "The balloon was designed poorly."

"There were flaws," Passepartout said. "But they did work. Had I had more time, more experimentation, those problems would not have occurred."

Ned began writing.

THERE ARE SCIENTISTS IN AMERICA WHO FIXED IT SO BUFFALO BILL COULD LIVE ONLY AS A HEAD IN A JAR. THEY ARE SMART. I REMEMBER SOME NAMES. MORSE. PROFESSOR MAXXON.

Beadle nodded. "We may need them as well. But for now, we have Steam, and we have a new mission. John Feather and I, we are soldiers of a sort, and we are at our best when battling for the common good. So we look forward to being put ashore."

"These Martians," Twain said. "They have the machines, but they also have a kind of...what would you call it, Verne?"

"Ray," Verne said. "A beam of light that destroys."

"The machines are fast, and they are strong," Passepartout said. "So my friends, you will be in for a fight."

"We're ready," John Feather said. "We've no place to go back to, really. No way to get back if we could. Our friends are dead. We have new friends here. We are ready to do what we can. Besides, you saved our lives. We owe you."

"I intend to prove that Frenchmen are as brave as anyone on the face of the earth," Verne said.

"Oui, Oui," Passepartout said.

Ned wrote:

I HAVE SEEN THE MARTIANS. I SAW THEM THROUGH THE GLASS IN FRONT OF THEIR MACHINES. THEY LOOK LIKE AN OCTOPUS. I SAW A DEAD ONE. HE HAD TWO ASSHOLES.

"That's true," Twain said. "Very much so."

Ned wrote some more.

WE WOULD BE JUST LIKE IN THE DIME NOVELS. PALS, WORKING TOGETHER TO DESTROY THE BAD GUYS. THE BAD OCTOPUSSES. OCTOPUSSY. OCTOPIE. YOU KNOW WHAT I MEAN.

"We do," John Feather said.

Ned wrote again.

YOU KNOW, I MIGHT COULD EAT A MARTIAN. I LIKE OCTOPUS.

"I think I'd let that one go," Verne said. "You don't know where they've been."

"Mars," Twain said.

"Yes," Verne said, "but where on Mars? They could have some very vulgar habits, you know. They could live up an animal's ass or roll in shit or eat it by the pound. We don't know a thing about them."

"You don't know anything about Martians," Twain said. "They could be very clean."

Rikwalk appeared, rubbing his eyes.

"Sorry," he said, "all that work at the booze wheel has exhausted me."

"That's all right," Twain said. "I've been thinking about you speaking

English, trying to come up with a reason. But all it does is make my head hurt."

"I believe that at one point in time, explorers from Earth were on Mars," Verne said. "Perhaps when Mars was in its infancy. I have even thought that apes from Earth may have come with the Earthlings. For experimentation, I'm afraid. The apes were perhaps advanced, maybe even modified to speak. They learned English. Perhaps they mated with an indigenous Martian species, and you, my friend, are the results."

Rikwalk nodded. "I suppose that is possible. The Earth we know is an empty world. Dried up and burned up by the heat of the sun. Our scientists have suggested a collapsed ozone layer, but no one knows. There is a theory that apes came from manlike beings, or that their genetics were somehow entwined with ours, but again, no one knows this for a fact. Man, on our world, does not exist. Just their bones. We, of course, have people who have studied this extensively, as well as our language, and at some point in time, it just seems as if we came into existence. And, though there is evidence of man, it has long been assumed that he was our inferior ancestor. From the reconstructions I've seen in museums, you beings look much like those reconstructions. Though there are some differences."

"Like what?" Twain asked.

"We had no idea that you were...mostly hairless. We assumed that you had a mild coat of hair."

"What I would like to know is why our Martians have invaded our Earth?" Passepartout said.

"The reason all invaders invade," Twain said. "Greed."

"Perhaps their world is dying," Verne said.

"White Man kill Indian cause him want land," Bull said. "Him fuck up land. Shit-eating white bastards."

"I do not think he means you," Cat said.

"After what I saw him do with that knife to those pirates," Twain said, "I certainly hope not."

Bull made a grunting noise. It could have meant anything.

"I believe," the Dutchman said, "we are coming to a good place to set ashore. I'm going to need all hands, including passengers, to help. So, all hands alive."

Ninteeen

On Shore, a Hunt for Fuel, Separated, Horrible Events

There were great white birds everywhere, and they screamed at the sky and soared above the sails. A black bird, perhaps a crow, appeared, fluttered and landed atop the center mast.

"Not a good sign," Twain said.

He and Verne were working at pulling ropes, lowering a sail to the command of one of the Dutchman's mates.

"On this ship," Verne said, "I would assume that bad signs are consistent, considering the captain and his crew are doomed."

"Question is," Twain said, "does his curse extend to us? Are we now part of his crew?"

"I hadn't thought of that," Verne said. "I hope that if there was a curse, it applies only to those who were with the Dutchman's ship at the time he seduced this witch's daughter. And could be the Dutchman is no more doomed or cursed than you or I, except in his mind."

"Could be," Twain said. "But I'll be glad to leave this ship, nonetheless."

The ship edged toward shore, and when they were some distance out, a great rope was attached to the bow of the ship, and Rikwalk dropped over the side, grabbing the rope, first swimming, finally wading toward shore, pulling the great ship forward. His strength was remarkable, like that of an elephant.

Twain and Verne watched this event. Twain said, "I'm glad he's on our side."

—————

Rikwalk pulled the ship to shore. Those who wished to disembark did so. In the cruiser came Verne, Twain, Ned, Passepartout. The cruiser floated over the side of the ship, dropping down, blowing over the water near the shore, and finally onto land itself.

Beadle and John Feather disembarked inside of Steam.

Steam, puffing and wheezing, strode down the gangplank. He walked through the shallows and onto the shore, stood there in the sunlight, shiny as a fresh minted coin, a coil of steam slowly vaporizing around his head.

Bull and Cat waved to those on the shore from the ship.

"Keep powder dry," Bull called, placing his arm around Cat.

"You too, my friend," Passepartout called.

Inside Steam, Beadle and John Feather caused the metal man's arm to lift, and with a creaking noise, wave good-bye.

The Dutchman called out, "Good luck, friends. And now, if you would be so kind, Rikwalk."

Rikwalk took hold of the rope and pulled, tugging the bow of the ship around. He pulled the ship out to sea. When it was as deep as he could go, when the water was up to his armpits, he let go of the rope, swam behind the ship and pushed. When the ship was moving comfortably on its own, Rikwalk swam back to shore, shook himself and joined the others, stood beside Steam. He was almost as tall as Steam, but the metal man's conical hat stood ten feet higher than Rikwalk's head.

Rikwalk leaned forward and pressed his face against the stained glass eyes. That way he could look inside, see Beadle and John Feather at the controls. They waved at him, said, "Pee-Pie," as he moved his face away.

John Feather turned to Beadle said, "Man, that was some creepy shit. A big ape eye looking in on us."

"I'm glad he's on our side," Beadle said.

⸺◆⸺

As they watched the ship sail away, the sky turned dark and split wide open, making a tall, wide, purple wound. And before you could say, Holy Shit! Look out, goddamnit! the Dutchman's ship sailed through the crack in the sky and out of sight, as if falling off the face of the world.

The split did not widen.

And it did not close.

"It's worsening," Beadle said from inside Steam. "This world will soon be like ours."

"Bless them," John Feather said.

After watching for a long time in astonishment, the split did close. Slowly, as if curtains were being pulled together.

The gang was torn up about it, but knew there was nothing they could do. After a few words of complaint, a cry of lament, they decided to get on with things.

"We don't know that where they went is bad," said Twain.

"That's true," said Verne. "They could be anywhere."

"But it could be bad," Passepartout said.

"Yes," Verne said. "It could."

Ned, though distraught at what might be happening to his friends, Bull and Cat, bucked up and took a dip in the ocean to dampen himself, as well as nab a couple of fat fish. When he was finished with that, they started on their journey.

—⬥—

It was suggested by Beadle, and decided by the group, that everyone, with the obvious exception of Rikwalk, would ride inside of Steam. It was not a gentle ride. Beadle and John Feather sat in spring loaded seats and worked the controls, and when Steam stepped, the whole machine jostled. There were a couple of hammock style seats in the machine, and Ned claimed one of them immediately. The other was tossed for. Twain won the toss. Verne and Passepartout made do with sitting on the floor near the controls.

Though being cautious was wise, and back roads were taken, hiding something the size of Rikwalk and Steam didn't seem likely. But neither did it seem smart to abandon such a machine, and, of course, there was no thought of abandoning a friend like Rikwalk.

As Steam strode along, Rikwalk walking beside the great machine, they could see that the road was littered with the bodies of both humans and animals, horsedrawn transportation lay wrecked all about.

Inside Steam, Twain said, "I'm all for a fight. I want to fight. We have to fight. But maybe walking right into their midst isn't such a good idea. And now that I think about it, I really don't want to fight that bad."

Ned wrote: WE CAN HIDE OUT LIKE RATS IN THE COUNTRYSIDE. THAT MIGHT BE A GOOD IDEA.

"You're right," Verne said. "We can't act like rats. We're men."

NO. I WASN'T KIDDING. I MEANT IT. LET'S HIDE LIKE RATS. AND I'M A SEAL.

"What I am thinking," Verne said, "is we make it to London, try and find Herbert. He is a smart man, and has access to a lot of scientific equipment. Perhaps together, and with the aid of all who are present, we can come to some conclusion as to how these invaders can be defeated."

"Who's Herbert?" Beadle asked.

"Herbert Wells," Verne said. "H. G. Wells. The writer and scientist. A good friend of mine."

"I'll be damned," Beadle said.

"What?" Verne asked.

"Well," Beadle said. "He's a writer on our world as well. But not a scientist.

"And I don't know if you and Samuel know one another on our world. Or even if you know Mr. Wells. In fact, I think the timing is a little off. I'm not sure. I'm no expert on such things. But there is much overlap between your world and ours. We too have invaders. Saucer machines. They came through the rips. They're just one of many problems. I'm afraid it may be too late for our world; too many rips, too many invaders. But if we can't get back to our home, can't save it, perhaps we can save this world."

Ned wrote: YOU TALK A LOT LIKE A DIME NOVEL.

Beadle grinned. "If you say so."

"We are going to have to find fuel soon," John Feather said. "And I suggest after we make a bit of mileage, we stop for the day, hide out, and travel by night. We're less likely to be discovered that way."

"I agree," Verne said.

The others chimed in in agreement.

Ned made a noise that sounded somewhere between a burp and bark. Later, lying there in the hammock, he tried to squeeze out a silent fart, but didn't make it. It burst out like a foghorn blast.

Ned wrote: EXCUSE ME.

They went on for many miles, fanning Ned's fart, trekking down a back road, and finally they came to a forested area. Light was seeping out of the day like water running through fingers. They walked Steam off the road, inside a grove of trees, geared him down. They got out and went looking for wood to stoke the furnace.

"We'll need a good supply," Beadle said. "It's a long trek, it takes a lot to maintain steam power. Night is falling, so we must hurry. And for a time it is nice to be free of the gas in the machine."

Ned wrote:

I'M SORRY. I SAID I WAS SORRY. WHAT MORE CAN I DO?

They split into wood search groups.

It was decided that Rikwalk, the strongest, was to stay and protect Steam, and to serve as a lookout.

Rikwalk pulled up a small tree, beat the dirt out of the roots, peeled off limbs with his bare hands, made a club of it. Then, with the club across his knees, he sat with his back to a great oak and waited, lost in his thoughts, spinning out happy scenarios of home, his job, his wife.

"Are you all right, Rikwalk?" Beadle asked.

"I am as good as I can be. At least I am among friends. But I think of home. My family. My job. My life. I miss it. I wonder if I will ever return to it. I'm not even on a version of my own world, but another world. You are at least on your own world."

"Not exactly," Beadle said. "In many ways, it's just as alien here for me and John Feather as it is for you. Buck up as best you can, my friend."

Beadle left Rikwalk, and joined John Feather. Verne and Passepartout formed a team as well. The gathering commenced.

———⇒·◦·⇐———

Twain decided that he would start a pile, gather good dead wood and then have Steam and Rikwalk come into the forest to get it. The way the trees grew, there was path enough for the big machine and the great ape, and it beat hauling it back in shifts.

Ned, dismounted from the cruiser, could only carry a few sticks in his mouth at a time, so it was a tedious process, him wriggling about.

But Twain couldn't help but admire the dauntless seal's efforts. He knew the debris of the forest floor had to hurt Ned's belly, but the seal did not complain.

As they searched for dead wood, without realizing it, Twain and Ned ventured some distance from the others and from the pile Twain had made. Just as Twain was about to turn back with his armload of wood, he noted that the woods had thinned, and a farmhouse and barn could be seen, surrounded by a rock fence. Twain said, "I don't know about you, Ned, but I'm so hungry I could eat shit and call it gravy."

Ned wrote: I DON'T WANT SHIT TO CALL GRAVY, BUT I COULD EAT SOME FISH. I COULD EAT MOST ANYTHING. EXCEPT SHIT.

"I believe you're taking me a bit too literally."

I WOULD REALLY HAVE TO BE HUNGRY TO EAT SHIT. GODDAMN HUNGRY. I'M PRETTY HUNGRY NOW, BUT NOT GODDAMN HUNGRY. I DO NOT WANT SHIT.

"Got you. No shit."

Twain dropped the wood. "If we can find someone here, someone who will help us, supply food for our journey, it could be just as valuable, maybe more valuable than the wood. Let's have a look around, Ned."

Ned clapped his flippers together and barked.

⋙•◆•⋘

They trekked back to where they had left the cruiser, and mounted up. From the woods to the farmhouse was a short trip by cruiser. Upon nearing it, they were shocked to discover that a portion of the house and the stone wall had been blown away.

"The machines, they've been here," Twain said. "We should look for survivors."

They left the cruiser outside, went inside the house and looked. Nothing.

They used the cruiser to check the grounds and the barn. No one.

"Perhaps they got away."

Ned wrote: OR GOT ALL MELTED. DON'T SEE ANY CHICKENS EITHER. HOGS. WHAT HAVE YOU.

"Ah," Twain said. "A dead horse."

Sure enough, behind a hedge row lay a horse, bloated, dead, and stinky.

"I suppose we could have some horse meat, but I don't know, it looks a little—"

Ned was writing:

RANK AS THE ASS END OF A WALRUS. I'M NOT EATING THAT.

"Have no fear, Ned. We will only eat fresh horse."

I COULD EAT A DOG.

"Hopefully it won't come to that."

OR A CAT. IF IT IS COOKED RIGHT.

———✦———

Back in the house they found a bag of flour and a bag of sugar. There were some dried meats and some canned goods, but little else. When Twain opened a cabinet, he leaped back. A body tumbled out.

It was a little girl, about six. She was starting to rot away. She was still in the position in which she had died, clutching her knees, her head bent.

"My God," Twain said. "She must have crawled in there to hide, was too frightened to come out. She sat in there until she starved. My God, what she must have seen. How horrible it must have been. Can you imagine being so frightened you would rather starve?"

PERHAPS SHE DIED OF FRIGHT.

"I suppose that's possible. Poor thing. We must bury her, Ned. I'll go out to the barn, see if I can find a shovel."

YOU'RE NOT LEAVING MY ASS HERE. I'M GOING WITH YOU.

They went out to the barn on the cruiser. They found a shovel. Twain eyed a wheelbarrow, and some dried vegetables hanging from the rafters.

"If we use the wheelbarrow, we can haul some of these vegetables, the flour and sugar, back to Steam."

WHY NOT JUST PUT IT IN THE CRUISER?

"We will pack the cruiser as well, but I suggest we take all we can. There's room in Steam for a lot of stuff, and who knows when we'll need it.

"First, we'll take care of that poor child. My God, it makes me think of my own tragic family."

I AM SO SORRY.

"Me too, Ned. Life just keeps throwing darts."

BUT WE KEEP DODGING.

"You are one remarkable seal, my friend."

THANKS. YOU ARE NOT SO BAD YOURSELF. ARE YOU GOING TO WRITE ANYMORE ABOUT HUCKLEBERRY FINN? OTHER THAN THE ONE WHERE THEY GO TO AFRICA BY BALLOON. I DON'T COUNT THAT ONE.

"Not your meat, I take it."

I REALLY THOUGHT IT BIT THE HIND END OF A MOOSE. BUT I SURE LIKED *HUCKLEBERRY FINN* AND *TOM SAWYER.* I LIKED *THE PRINCE AND THE PAUPER.* I LIKED *A CONNETICUT YANKEE IN KING ARTHUR'S COURT.* HAVE YOU EVER THOUGHT ABOUT WRITING A BOOK ABOUT A SEAL?

Ned paused to erase and write again.

I WOULD READ A BOOK ABOUT A SEAL. I THINK A LOT OF PEO-PLE WOULD. I THINK IT WOULD SELL A LOT. SEALS ARE INTEREST-ING. I CAN BE FUNNY TOO. I KNOW SOME JOKES.

"It's something I will consider seriously, Ned. And, yes, seals are interesting. Later, I can hear your jokes. But for now, let us go back to the house and attend to this rather dreary duty."

⊰◈⊱

Back in the farmhouse, Ned pulled a blanket off of a bed with his teeth and dragged it into the kitchen area where the little girl lay. Twain, using the shovel because the body was too decayed to touch, rolled the little corpse onto the blanket. He wrapped the blanket around the body, and Ned jerked down some curtain cord with his strong teeth, and Twain tied up the ends of the blanket.

Gently, Ned holding the blanket in his teeth at one end, Twain lifting it at the other, they carried the corpse outside. Twain started to dig.

It was hard there, and there were plenty of small stones. It took considerable time to dig a grave deep enough to contain the body, and by the time Twain finished, he was covered in sweat, his great mane of hair plastered to his head like a tight bathing cap.

They lowered the unfortunate victim into the confines of the earth, then, with Twain using the shovel and Ned pushing dirt in with his flippers, they covered her up.

Ned used his flippers to push some of the rocks into a pile, to form a sort of makeshift marker at one end of the grave.

"Sleep well, darling. May angels attend thee. Even though I doubt there are any, and if there are, they're nasty little shits and God is a malign thug."

THAT WAS A VERY NICE CEREMONY. YOU ARE NOT A RELIGIOUS MAN, ARE YOU?

"Not when God allows children to die. Mine or any other. God can kiss my ass."

THAT'S NOT VERY NICE.

"I suppose not."

IT IS A VERY DIRTY ASS RIGHT NOW.

Twain turned, brushed dirt from the seat of his pants. It had collected there during the two breaks he had taken while digging the grave, sitting with his back to the fence.

"Well, Ned. We should gather our goods and try and find our friends and Steam. It is growing dark."

Ned made a noise, a barking sound.

"What, Ned?"

Ned clapped his flippers.

"What?"

Ned wrote:

BIG GODDAMN MARTIAN MACHINE.

Twain looked over his shoulder. And sure enough, stalking between the house and the woods was a machine, striding about like a three-legged spider. From that distance, they could not see the Martians behind the view glass clearly, but they could see bloblike shapes working the controls.

"In the house, quick, Ned."

They leaped onto the cruiser and geared it toward the house. The house wall was torn open on one side from previous Martian attacks, so it was easy for them to glide inside.

They collapsed the machine and rolled it against the wall near a bedroom window at the back. Then, sitting to the side of the bed, their backs to the wall, they listened.

It was then that they heard the sound of guns in the distance. "My God, the British are fighting back," Twain said.

This thundering went on for a time, shaking the cottage, causing the window to jar so fiercely, for a moment it seemed as if it would break free of its moorings.

Eventually, Twain rose, and leaving Ned to wait in the bedroom, slipped into the kitchen, where the wall was broken down.

Out in the dark, Twain could see the machine stalking about, a light glowing from its head and flashing over the landscape. The head wheeled on its gears and sockets, and the light shot out in Twain's direction.

Jumping back, Twain hoped he had not been spotted. He crouched low against what remained of the kitchen wall, half expecting a ray to strike and cause the whole thing to crumble down in a heap on top of him.

The light rotated away, and Twain eased his head around the broken wall for a peek. The machine was stomping off into the darkness. He was glad to see that it was not moving toward the woods where the others and Steam waited.

Back in the bedroom, Twain briefly and quietly reported to Ned what he had seen. There was the continuous sound of gunfire now, and it seemed to be moving closer, as if being pushed along by a current. Then, abruptly, the thundering of guns stopped.

Looking out the window, Twain saw a strange sight. A white mist appeared to be rising out of the distance. He could see it clearly in the moonlight, and soon it was like a gossamer gown thrown over the face of the moon.

"Smoke," Twain said. "Explosions. And now silence. I fear the Martians have knocked out the gun batteries. The goddamn shit-eating dick-sucking bastards."

WAS THAT ONE WORD?

"No."

WHAT NOW?

"Our only recourse is to return to Steam. Taking our goods with us.

I'm going to look about in the house a bit more. Living out here in the country, perhaps there is a bird gun."

Twain looked about, but found nothing of the sort.

———

Outside, Twain took hold of the wheelbarrow handles and started to push. Ned mounted the cruiser, which was also packed with goods, and floated alongside of him.

To the north, they could see not only smoke now, but great fires, and there were distant cries as well.

"The machines are winning," Twain said.

———

At the edge of the woods, Twain found pushing the wheelbarrow a hard go. The ground was too mushy. He managed it to the spot where they had left the pile of wood and stopped. "I'm leaving it here," Twain said. "We can get Steam to come for the wood and the barrow. There's a path here. It might be tight, but he can make it. I'm all tuckered out."

Twain climbed on the cruiser, and Ned geared it along the trail, toward where they had left their friends, and Steam.

But when they arrived on the far edge of the woods, near the road, neither Steam nor their friends were about.

Lying in the road with its legs bent and twisted and broken was one of the Martian Machines. The club Rikwalk had made for himself was stuffed through what had been the face glass of the machine.

Twain climbed down from the cruiser, went over for a look. It was dark, but near the machine lay a Martian. It looked as if something had taken hold of it and squeezed until what was inside of it had come out the top of its head.

Steam.

———

Ned slid the cruiser over close to Twain. He wrote: WHY DID THEY LEAVE?

"I don't know," Twain said. "But they wouldn't have left us had they not had to. My guess is, from all the marks in the road here, the place was swarming with machines. Steam got this Martian and Rikwalk got the machine. And then they fled. It was the smart thing to do. I would have done the same. They were most likely outnumbered."

Ned slapped a flipper to his side, pointed with the other.

Lying in the woods was another machine. Twain climbed onto the cruiser, and they glided over for a look.

This machine had been bent up too, and this Martian pilot had suffered the same fate as his partner. He lay near the machine, part of his body draped over a log.

"Steam just reached inside the glass, took him out like a baby grabbing a chocolate," Twain said. "Then, he squeezed him."

IS THAT MARTIAN SHIT HANGING OUT OF HIS TWO ASSHOLES?

"I doubt it's flour gravy, Ned."

THEIR SHIT IS THE WRONG COLOR.

"I suppose they might say the same about ours. And my guess is that shit is mixed with a lot of other things. Blood. His guts. And we're seeing it in moonlight...I can't believe I'm standing out here discussing Martian shit with a seal."

WHAT DO WE DO?

"We go on."

INTO THAT MESS.

Ned pointed a flipper down the road. At the far end of it and beyond there were great red and yellow flames lapping at the darkness with the enthusiasm of a hound licking an ice cream cone.

"I suppose we must find our friends. They will be worried about us. They might even circle about to find us."

"They think you're dead."

Ned and Twain whirled at the sound of the voice.

The speaker came staggering out of the woods holding his head with one hand, a rifle with the other. It was Jules.

Twain leaped from the cruiser, grabbed his old friend, who suddenly collapsed to the ground.

"Jules. My God, man, what happened?"

"As you might suspect, the machines, my friend."

"Where are the others?"

"Gone on. We were looking for wood, then we were looking for you."

"We were detained by a machine. Ned and I were trapped in a farmhouse. We had supplies. But then we found this business."

"They came on us suddenly. Steam was stoked up, though. Wood had been brought back and there was a fire in his belly. Or wherever the damn fire is. The machines saw us. Rikwalk took to them. He scampered up the side of one, tugged it down by hanging off it, letting his weight take it to the ground. He shoved a tree into it.

"Steam stomped the machine, grabbed the Martian out. Steam and Rikwalk got another one before the others came. Ten machines. Rikwalk and I decided we would detain them. There was a rifle in Steam. I took that and dropped out. The others were reluctant that we should do what we intended, but Rikwalk and I wanted them to go on. Passepartout knows how to reach Herbert. Herbert is the only reason to go to London. He is the only one who might save us. Our very planet. Either him, or Professor Challenger, if he can be found. But we sent them on. Rikwalk and I scampered into the woods, and the machines tried to follow. A ray was shot at me. It missed, but it hit a tree near me and the tree fell and I was hit.

"I don't know why I wasn't finished off. Maybe they thought I was dead. All I remember was hearing Rikwalk yelling at them. Trying to get them after him. I passed out. Then I awoke to the sound of your voice, Samuel. I have no idea what happened to Rikwalk. But I fear the worst."

"If Wells is our best bet," Twain said, "I suppose we too should head that way, into London. If Steam doesn't make it, then we must. And frankly, being a smaller target may work to our advantage."

"Agreed."

There was a little first-aid kit inside the cruiser, and Twain, using the meager resources of that kit, bandaged Verne's head.

Then, with Ned at the controls, they were off.

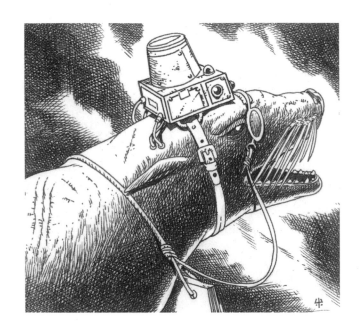

Twenty

Ned's Journal: Flaming London, Reunion, We Take a Captive of Sorts

The great fire before us made London seem near. But it was not. In fact, it was not only London that burned, but much that surrounded it. We cruised silently through many a charred village. Humans and animals lay littered about like tossed garbage. Carts and other vehicles were crushed and burning, and homes were often little more than rubble. There was a stink that rose up from the dead that was almost unbearable. Fish, when rotting, do not smell that bad, and in fact, rotting fish, if dipped briefly in sea water, and then eaten, really aren't that bad.

We had food in the cruiser that we had taken from the farmhouse. It was simple but acceptable under the circumstances. There had been a couple tins of dried fish in the wheelbarrow we had left in the woods, but neither Mr. Twain nor Mr. Verne wanted to go back after it.

I wanted to go back after it, but they overruled me. Sometimes democracy is not all it is cracked up to be.

But there were some potted meats and some dried cheeses that stank, and we ate that with some bread near hard as hammers, and drank water from a bottle Mr. Twain had taken from the farmhouse. It was better than sticking a sharp stick up your ass and cranking it, but only a little better. In fact, if you could grease that stick with butter, it might even have been the better deal.

We spent several days traveling, and along the way we encountered a couple of destroyed Martian machines.

"Steam," Mr. Verne said. "He got some more."

"He's been lucky to miss the rays," Mr. Twain said.

"He didn't always miss them," Mr. Verne said. "I saw him lose one of his metal fingers to one, right before I bolted into the woods. He's as fast as the Martian machines. It's really quite remarkable."

"When they get to London, what are they going to do? Put him in their pockets? They can hardly sneak about with that big tin man."

"I have no idea," Mr. Verne said. "But Beadle and John Feather, and my good friend Passepartout, they are resourceful."

"No doubt."

———⊷·⊶———

We traveled by night and slept by day. Sometimes we slept in the woods, or down in gullies, and on occasion in abandoned or near-destroyed farmhouses.

Finally one morning, just as light was slipping through the shadows, we came to signs that told us we were on the outskirts of London. I would normally have been excited. I have always heard of, and have of course read much of London. But now I knew there would be nothing fine to see. From where we stood, was a view of black churning smoke and spits of flames, and even from that distance, the smell of death.

"We should find a place to hole up for the day, and even the night," Mr. Twain said. "We need to be rested. Tomorrow we make London. Such as it is."

———⊷·⊶———

We did find a place. A small grove of trees. It was comfortable enough, and we slept away the day, awakening at nightfall.

It was decided we wouldn't travel this night, or the next day. Instead, we would rest, eat plenty of food before proceeding on our journey.

We had a cold supper of canned meat, hard bread and water. There was little water left in the container, and it was decided, though it was dark, that we should venture out of the grove and cross over into the village to look for water.

On this last night before entering London, we had chosen to sleep outside the village for the simple reason that at night the Martian machines roamed such places looking for survivors. But with our water running low, and me needing a rubdown and feeling dehydrated, we took the cruiser back into town, came to a house where we found a water pump and were able to fill our bottle and douse me good.

We had no sooner accomplished that than we heard movement amongst a pile of ruins not far from us. Mr. Verne had the rifle Beadle had given him, a kind of scoop-cocking affair that Mr. Twain said resembled an American Winchester. He lifted it and listened.

No doubt about it. Something was moving amongst the debris near us, behind what remained of the ray blasted walls. And it sounded huge.

We scampered back onto the cruiser and glided behind the remains of a cottage. Mr. Twain leaned out from the edge of the wall for a peek.

"My God," he said.

"What is it?" Mr. Verne said.

"Ned, bring the cruiser out into the open."

I hesitated for only a moment, then did as Mr. Twain instructed. Coasting out from behind the cottage I saw a wonderful sight, and even though my vision was clouded by night, there was enough light from the stars and the scattered fires from the burning village for me to know exactly what I was seeing.

Rikwalk, squatting, staring at us. When he saw us, he let out a whelp and came running, thundering along on back legs and front knuckles. In that moment he looked like nothing more than a huge gorilla.

As he came to the cruiser, he snatched Mr. Twain out of it, hugged him, set him on the ground, then did the same with Mr. Verne. I was third. Grabbed from the floating cruiser and hugged furiously, he placed me back gently behind the controls.

Mr. Twain and Mr. Verne remained on the ground. Mr. Twain said, "My god, you are all right. We feared the worst."

"And so you should have. But here I am."

"Come, let us go back to our place in the grove," Mr. Verne said. "We can talk there. We have food."

————⧓————

"So when they came, and I saw they were after you, I yelled to them, and they came after me—"

"And I thank you for that, my brother," Mr. Verne said. "It was a brave and noble thing to do."

"No. Not at all. You would have done the same. I ran, and they pursued. I went deep into the woods. On our world, my Mars, there is much foliage, and we use it to travel from place to place. There are even nets amongst the great trees for lounging, and many of our people go there for leisure, and there are homes built there as well. I live in such a place, not far from the locks where I work...worked. So I felt right at home. Except the trees are smaller...And it wasn't home."

Mr. Twain reached out and touched Rikwalk's huge hand. "Easy, friend. If there is a way for you to return to your Mars, we will help you do it. I promise that."

"I know," Rikwalk said.

"Please," Mr. Twain said. "Continue with your story."

"There isn't much to tell. They pursued me through the woods, firing their rays, knocking down trees, causing a fire. I found a creek bed, and though I'm large, it was deep enough that I was able to make some passage down it, and then scamper up and into the trees. High up, amongst a thick growth of leaves, I hid. Wondering if the tree I was in would be hit by one of their rays.

"It wasn't, but as the machines came through, one of them smashed against the tree where I hid, and the might of the machine caused it to shake, and then the machine, somehow standing on two of its metal tentacles, used the other tentacle to grab the tree, and the machine pulled it up by its roots and threw it."

"My God," Mr. Verne said.

"The tree went for some distance and came down hard.Fortunately, I was on the clear side of its fall, and I was spared. I thought it had been grabbed because they knew I was in it, but it seemed that they were merely clearing a path, and the tree I was in happened to be blocking it. I stayed there amongst its limbs until the machine and its companions departed. When I was sure they were gone, I slipped away and have been moving slowly toward the town you call London ever since. I followed the road from a distance, not traveling on it itself, going mostly by night, sleeping in the day, but keeping it in sight as a kind of guide."

Mr. Twain told him of our adventures, and when he was finished, he said, "We have decided to rest through this night, and all of tomorrow. Then when tomorrow night falls, we go into London. We felt, tired as we were, we should try and rest as much as possible. We have food. Can you use some?"

"I am famished, my friend. I found a number of canned goods, but I had to beat them open on a rock. A lot of the contents got splattered. I've mostly lived off bugs and worms, which, frankly, to me are a kind of delicacy, though I prefer them slow grilled in garrodo(6) fat."

"I will not even ask," Mr. Verne said.

Rikwalk grinned. We gave him the food we had left, and he polished it off greedily. With his belly as full as he could manage, and with half the water from our bottle in his stomach, he lay back and was immediately asleep.

It would have seemed that traveling by day, being up by night, we would not have been able to sleep as well. But it was quite the contrary. I lay next to the collapsed cruiser, and there, with a pile of leaves for a pillow, fell into a deep sleep. When I awoke, it was in the exact same position I had laid down, and my awakening was to the singing of birds and bright rays of sunlight lacing between the boughs of the trees.

The day was hot. I felt as if I were a dying bug specimen in a bottle, killing fumes rising up from the bottom of the bottle, the lid corked, and me with no place to go. Only the stink we encountered was not that of the killing jar, but that of the dead who lay bloated in the village and along the roadside.

It occurred to me, though I tried not to dwell on it, that odds were good that we might soon join them.

—◆—

We stayed in our grove most of the day, talking, trying to plan strategy, but there was little to plan. The obvious and smart thing to

---

6. A farm animal raised for meat and milk on Rikwalk's Mars.

have done would have been not to go into London, but to hide out and stay hidden.

But we were determined to reach Wells, and possibly find a way to get rid of these horrid invaders. We also spoke of Bull and Cat, the Dutchman, his ship and crew. Where were they? Had they lived through their traveling to another world? Was it another Earth? Mars? Hell? Would we ever know?

And what of Beadle and John Feather and Passepartout, the big machine they called Steam?

Had they traveled by night?

Could they have sneaked into London?

Finally, that sort of talk and consideration died out and we began to talk about things that had nothing to do with our current situation. Twain talked of his losses, and how his humor had almost dried up. Verne talked of frustration with his publisher, how they did not want him to publish a very dark novel he was writing about Paris. Rikwalk talked of his family, his world, and how he missed it. He spoke so elo-quently, when he finished, I missed his Mars as well.

And I spoke of fish.

I know. It's a simple thing. But I like fish. I think about them all the time. I was also hot, and at some point we made our way back to the village and watered me down with the pump, filled our water bot-tle, and managed to find a few tins of food. We carried these back to the grove, and waited there until nightfall. Talking. Eating. Dozing. Dreaming. Fearing.

⟐

And so the night came and we started out. Rikwalk knuckled alongside the cruiser, and we hovered over the countryside, not far from the road, ever on the lookout for the machines.

About the same time that night fell, a fog rose. It misted whitely across the land as if it were some kind of mystical dragon. It seemed to coil and writhe over the landscape. Soon, we found ourselves inside it, wrapped up by it, and once again, I thought of those insect specimens balled up in cotton, waiting for death.

I thought, would it be so bad to return to the sea?

Out there I could live free.

I couldn't keep my hat, since it wouldn't last in the sea, or stay on my head for two shakes. But I would be amongst my own kind. Except for the fact that they would not be as smart and wouldn't have books and the metalwork on my head, though resistent to rust in general, might be ruined by too much water and too much salt.

It was a hard thing to consider.

No fez.

No books.

But there would be fish.

My thoughts were exploded when Rikwalk whispered.

"There. See the light?"

And we did. It was high up and fanning about. The light from the head of one of the Martian killing machines.

There was a hill in front of us, and we went tight against it. I settled the cruiser down on the ground, and we stood inside it.

Rikwalk lay down on the ground and rolled on his side, let his back rest against the base of the hill. It was the only way he could not be conspicuous.

There were dead sheep lying about the hill, under the fog, as if it were their blanket. They had been hit by rays and were missing heads and limbs and had head-sized holes punched through them. The holes were clean and cauterized. The Martians, not distinguishing the sheep from humans, had destroyed them along with everything else in their path. They were bloated and bug-infested, and they stunk to high heaven, and the fog held the stink down close to the earth.

The machine was on the other side of the hill and above us, slicing into the fog. We could see its light. Then we could see more lights. I kept my flipper close to the cruiser's controls, lest we should need to spurt away.

Of course, the cruiser, though reasonably fast, was nowhere near as swift as the stalking machines, but it was more maneuverable. I tried to keep that in mind as we waited and trembled. At least I was trembling. I don't know about the others.

One of the tentacled metal legs stepped over our hill, made us gasp for breath. The leg almost came down on top of us. And then the machine stepped again, bringing forward its other legs. It scuttled like an amputee spider. We stayed pressed against the hill. Soon, above it, there appeared three flying wedge-like crafts with big bright red lights in the front of them.

"My God," Verne said. "They have new machines. They've got flying machines. They look to be two or three-seater crafts for those big octopusses. Ocotopussies. Octopi. Whatever."

I wrote and held it close to my companions so they could see it. Well, I don't know if they actually could see it there in that foggy darkness, but it made me feel good to write it.

LOOKS LIKE WE'RE FUCKED. WHO'S FOR GOING BACK TO THE SEA? SHOW OF HANDS. WHAT SAY WE FIND A TROPICAL ISLAND WITH SEXUALLY WILLING SEALS? NATIVE GIRLS FOR YOU GUYS. RIKWALK, I GUESS YOU GET TO FUCK A MONKEY.

"We're not dead yet," Twain said, either in response to my note, or just because he thought it was appropriate.

I'm sure that could change at a moment's notice.

"Come on, they've passed us," Twain said. "We should move forward."

⸺⸱⸺

I don't know how we made it, since we saw numerous stalking machines that night. The flying wedges as well. But I suppose the fog, which was at first a nuisance, turned out to be our ally.

Well before daylight we arrived on the outskirts of London, no worse for wear, except in the department of exhaustion, due primarily to fear. Rikwalk showed no signs of exhaustion, and unlike us, who had been riding, he had been under his own power.

But he did show sadness. The look on his face, illuminated by burning London buildings, was enough to make me cry. Which, strangely enough, is an ability I've acquired. Maybe it has something to do with the way Doctor Momo wired my brain. But there have been many changes in me since the old days, which, frankly, are harder and harder for me to remember. I do remember quite well my preoccupation with fish. That hasn't changed much.

I still think about seal nookie as well.

I think that's healthy. Don't you?

We glided into London, staying close to the ruins of the city—for much of it now appeared to be ruins. Now and then we would see a human dart out from behind a wrecked building, cross our path with a wild glance, then disappear like a roach into a building across the way.

"Mankind is on the run," Mr. Twain said.

The sun rose and bathed us in morning light. Under other circumstances I would have found it beautiful, but for now I wanted back the night. I even welcomed the fog we had lost just outside of London. Now all our natural cover was gone.

Just as we turned a corner, trying to make our way down an alley, we saw one of the machines scampering along after us, flaming sunlight at its back.

Rikwalk said, "Go. I'll handle this. Give me the weapon, Mr. Verne."

Mr. Verne, without really thinking, handed him the rifle he had taken out of Steam. It was practically swallowed by Rikwalk's hand.

Rikwalk, sticking the rifle crosswise in his teeth, grabbed the wall of one of the buildings with his strong hands, climbed up hand over hand and foot over foot like...Well, he climbed like an ape. Rays blasted around him and bricks shattered and rained down on us.

We glided behind the building, down the alley. I didn't want to leave Rikwalk, but he had been so demanding, without thinking, I had done as he asked.

Above us, we heard the snap of the rifle, and then another snap. I looked back, and the machine had turned the corner and started toward us. But now, the glass that made up the windshield of the machine was shattered. I could see one of the creatures slumped over the gears, the other laboring to maintain his seat, green ichor spraying out of his head as if it were powered by a pump and firehose.

The machine dodged left, caught itself on one of its spidery legs, wobbled, wheeled, fell on its back with a smash.

I looked up. On the roof of the building was Rikwalk. He had the rifle in one of his hands, probably having fired it with his little finger; in his hands the rifle looked like a large toothpick.

"Hey," Rikwalk said, "I hit him. I don't know how, but I hit him."

"Come on down," Mr. Twain called.

———◆———

I geared the cruiser over there, and Mr. Twain and Mr. Verne leaped out and climbed on top of the machine. Behind the cracked glass lay the dead Martians. Again I was reminded of squid or octopuses...octopi...octopussies. Whatever. Nobody in our group could figure that multiple octopus thing out.

Anyway, the asswipes were dead.

Rikwalk climbed down, gave the rifle back to Mr. Verne.

"You are some shot," Verne said.

"I hate to admit this," Rikwalk said, "but the first time the weapon went off, total accident. Second time I just pointed. I can't believe I hit them. Both shots. Beginner's luck. Twice. It's the first piece of luck I've had since I scored with my wife before she was my wife. That's not for common knowledge by the way. We wouldn't want the kids to know that."

"We'll never speak a word, monsieur," Mr. Verne said.

"Here's the door," Mr. Twain said.

I eased the cruiser up and on top of the machine and glided over to where Mr. Twain was pointing. The machine lay on its side, and beneath it, where the legs were connected, was a sealed round doorway.

Mr. Verne climbed up there as well. He said, "Yes. It appears to be screwed on."

"There must be some way to unscrew it. If we could get inside, figure out the gears."

"Damn, Samuel, that could be a very good plan."

Rikwalk said, "Let's see."

With the tips of his fingers and his thumb, Rikwalk was able to turn the screw. The door came out like a plug.

Mr. Twain and Mr. Verne climbed inside. I could see them through the glass. The machine was wide enough they could stand up inside. They dragged the Martians out, tossed them on the ground.

Mr. Verne said, "I'm going to try and gear it up. See what happens."

"They had two at the controls," Mr. Twain said. "Maybe it takes two."

"Maybe so. We can try it. Ned. Will you come inside?"

I climbed off of the cruiser and collapsed it. With Rikwalk's help, (he shoved my ass with the palm of his hand) I wormed my way inside. He screwed the lid back onto the machine behind me.

Mr. Twain and Mr. Verne climbed into the strange chairs, which were designed for larger bodies, and lying sideways, they began to work the controls.

The spider legs thrashed, sending Rikwalk scuttling for cover. After a few trials, Mr. Verne was able to get one of the machine's legs bent and underneath itself, and with another push of a gear, the leg lifted the machine.

It immediately crashed on its side.

This event continued in repetition for a few moments, crashing hard enough that the already shattered glass shattered even more. Finally, a large chunk of it fell out.

I was being thrown around like some kind of ball, from side to side. My fez got knocked off, but I scrambled around until I recovered it.

I finally got hold of a grip bar on the side of the craft with my teeth, and held to it like I had hold of a whale.

Right then, I could have eaten a whale.

When I'm scared, I get hungry.

Frankly, I pretty much stay hungry.

After what seemed a little past forever, the machine stood. It wobbled at first, but in short time Mr. Twain and Mr. Verne had it. They stalked about the alley for a time, making the machine do different things. They slammed against the alley walls a bit, but before long they were operating it in a pretty smooth manner.

"It's actually simple," Mr. Twain said. "You just move these pegs the way you want it to go, and once you get it up, well, you point it in the direction you like with this gear, and it walks. You don't really need to work the legs individually then, unless you want them to do something specific. Like lift them tentacles higher, reach out and grab. That kind of business."

"That bit is worked with this," Mr. Verne said, touching another lever that moved side to side.

"It's kind of fun," Mr. Twain said.

Through the glass we could see Rikwalk. He grinned. "I think I should not stay too close to you. At a glance, you can pass as a Martian machine. I can not. Though, I might add, neither of you look like Martians."

We could hear Rikwalk well through the gaps in the glass. Mr. Twain called out, "Not looking like a Martian is a good thing in my book."

"Right now, it is better if you do look like one," Rikwalk said.

"Now," Mr. Verne said, "we find Herbert."

I wrote:

AND AFTER THAT, COULD WE FIND SOME FISH?

"Quite possible," Mr. Verne said. "And if not fish, food of some kind."

YIPPIE!!!!

Ned's journal ends.

Twenty-one

Big Ben, a Battle, Friends,
the Sky Gets Ripped

"We'll hide in plain sight," Twain said.

"How's that?" Verne said.

"Like in Poe's story, 'The Purloined Letter.' They couldn't find the letter, because it was not actually hidden. It was in plain sight. We can not only walk amongst the invaders, we will not be recognized."

"I think one good look at us and they'll know we're not Martians."

"Okay. It's not perfect, but it is a plan. I suggest that our next plan is to find out how the ray device on this works, how to aim it."

"And since you'll be doing that," Rikwalk said, "I'll climb on top of a building here."

Ned wrote:

AM I SAFE IN HERE FROM THE RAY?

"I should hope so," Twain said.

"Proceed toward the tower clock," Verne said to Rikwalk through the hole in the glass. "Herbert has a home and laboratory near there."

"I'm a little more conspicuous than you two," Rikwalk said.

"Oh, right you are," Verne said.

"I suggest you go directly to the tower if you can," Rikwalk said, "and I'll work my way there by whatever path I can find. It's a bit hard for an ape my size to stay out of sight."

After Rikwalk went up a wall, disappeared atop a building, Twain and Verne went about trying to find the device to work the ray. It didn't take long. They managed to blast down the side of the building Rikwalk had just vacated.

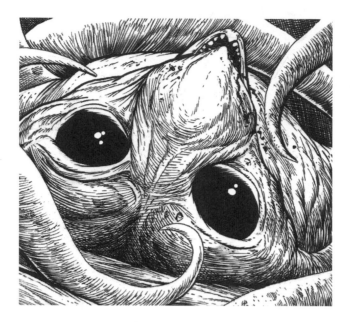

"I really didn't mean to do that," Verne said.

"I gathered," Twain said.

They worked with it a bit more, and soon they could aim it well enough, if not expertly. But they discovered they had the walking part down pretty well. They maneuvered the machine out of the alley and around the corner and out into the city proper.

In the distance, they could see the great tower clock, Big Ben. Ned glanced out and up, saw Rikwalk moving along a building top. Large as he was, he was moving quickly, shadowlike. Soon, he was out of sight.

"What say we point 'er at the big clock," Twain said, "and go."

———◆———

Many great Martian war machines hustled about the city, and our heroes went forward rapidly, trying not to get too close, trying to move in the direction of the tower as swiftly as possible, thinking Martian and hopefully looking Martian, but making sure they didn't get too close to their metal comrades so that they might be seen clearly through what remained of the view glass.

They saw a huge machine pause, turn its "head," and look at them.

It turned its glass-fronted noggin from side to side like a curious animal. The creatures behind the glass were practically pressed up against their windshield, trying to figure out what it was they were seeing.

—◦—

nickbic. that is not some of us, it is not. i can see that, i can. earth goobers. that is what we see, it is.

you are right, sumbuma. it is not what it should be, but is what it is. booger things. creepy things that walk this ground. they are in one of our machines.

greenless things. let's make them pretty like us. give them two assholes.

yuk, yuk, yuk.

going to melt them good, is what we are going to do. can I do it?

you did the last.

did not.

did too.

did not.

—◦—

They never finished their argument. Twain fired the ray from their machine, struck the Martian device solid. The windshield was knocked off whole. The machine twirled around on its legs so hard it practically braided them.

The machine went down.

"It was like before," Twain said. "They appeared to be quarreling."

Ned wrote:

QUARRELING CAN BE BENEFICIAL AND EVEN HEALTHY. BUT QUARRELING TOO MUCH, AND DURING TIMES OF STRESS AND IN TIMES OF NEED, IT CAN REALLY FUCK YOU UP. WITNESS THE MACHINE IN QUESTION. IT'S JUST SO MUCH JUNK NOW. IT IS BETTER NOT TO QUARREL. IT IS BETTER TO SIT DOWN OVER A DINNER OF FISH AND DISCUSS YOUR PROBLEMS. FEMALE SEALS ARE CONSIDERABLY MORE WILLING WHEN THEY HAVE FILLED THEIR BELLIES WITH FISH.

"I'll believe that," Twain said, working controls, helping the machine race down the street.

Other machines and their occupants had witnessed the destruction of one of their own machines by another, and now they were rushing toward our heroes.

Our heroes had the lead and—

———•◦•———

FIRST PHASE OF THE RACE
—they're off, and down the street they go, leaping, darting, weaving, and, oh shit, had to leap over some downed carts, and one tentacle went into a dead man's body, and that sucker is hung on the end of it now like a wad of chewy tobaccy on the bottom of a boot. It's throwing off our heroes a bit, and—

———•◦•———

SECOND PHASE OF THE RACE
—here they come, the Martians, and there are seven machines, and those green, multi-tentacled, two-assholed sonsabitches, they can really work those things. running their machines like goddamn deer, they are, closing, closing, closing—

———•◦•———

THIRD PHASE OF THE RACE
—four to the right, three to the left, and, with a shake of the tentacle, our heroes' machine is free of the dead body, and now Twain and Verne, they've got their gears pushed all the way forward, and they're working the balance controls, and whoopie, sudden stop, and—

———•◦•———

FOURTH PHASE OF THE RACE
—martian machines go, oh shit, because the humans (one assholed mother-father-uncle-aunt-hive-fuckers) have stopped short, and they have tried to stop short with them, and the results are the big double assed Martians are being smacked against their windshields.

squirty ass juice and sweaty nut balls, cries one.

One machine loses control, topples into another, their legs get entwined, down they go, thrashing about on the street and up against buildings like a stuck pig kicking out its last.

No time to help their comrades. they're down. way down. and frankly, they don't give a damn. they aren't big on sentiment.

Martians turn about angry, tentacles on those ray levers, baby, but the humans, they are gone. done took off like the proverbial and legendary spotted ass ape—

———

THE WINNERS!

—bounding along toward Big Ben they go, and inside the machine, Twain, he actually says, Wheeee!

———

Of course, it doesn't matter. The winner gets dick.

And the losers, they are not in a mood, so to speak.

And furthermore, or meanwhile, as is said in the story trade, our erstwhile heroes approach the tower clock, and right off they see there's good news, and there's bad news.

Good news:

Rikwalk, going his own way, over buildings, down side streets, sneaky as a Payute Indian in a war party, has made the tower clock. He's there.

That's the good part.

Now for the bad news:

Rikwalk has been seen. He's scuttling up the side of the tower, gripping a Martian by one of its legs. He has somehow broken into one of the machines (scuttled up it, smashed the glass with his fist, pulled out the Martian), and he's dragging the creature with him up the side of Big Ben.

He's a fast climber, Rikwalk is, and way up there he goes.

But there's more bad news.

Machines are closing in on him.

He works his way to the top of the tower, and there, holding the Martian, he begins to use the creature as a thrash rag, slinging him from side to side, bouncing him off of the clock tower, calling out names in English and in a language our heroes do not recognize.

Rays cut the air around him.

Zip. Zip. Zip.

Rikwalk can feel the hair on his body singeing, the rays are so close. He's so certain he's about to buy it, he can imagine his ancestral apes sitting on the limb of the great tree of life, dicks in one hand, the other over their eyes, their mouths open, but silent.

Rikwalk starts leaping up and down on the side of the clock, hanging on to it with one hand, dangling the Martian with the other, making primitive ape sounds.

"Ooohhh, oooohhhh, fucking shit. Ooohhhhh, oooohhhh. Eat my shit. Ooohhh, ooohhhh. Cocksucking octopussies."

———⊸•⊷———

"We've got to help him," Twain says.

Ned, who has his eye pressed against a smaller rear window turns, writes:

WE STILL HAVE MARTIAN MACHINES ON OUR TAIL.

"One thing at a time," Twain said.

———⊸•⊷———

Verne says, "Turn it. Quick."

And they do. Now they're facing the machines that are in pursuit. They fire rays. One of the machines takes a hit. It's charred on the side and part of the glass is melted out, but it keeps on coming.

The two that fell, they're still down, struggling to free their entwined tentacles.

A ray hits our heroes' machine.

It shakes. More of the glass falls out. Now there's just a sliver of glass in the right hand corner.

Ned thinks: Must think of happy moments. Fish. Fish. Fish. Nookie. Nookie. Nookie. Fish. Fish..."

"Turn it back," Twain says. "Run this thing like a bastard."

And they do. Sprinting their way toward the tower.

"We'll have Rikwalk leap on top of us when we get there," Twain said.

"I don't know that's such a good plan."

"You come up with another, let me know."

Their machine sprang across the vast expanse of bricks and cob-
blestones toward the tower; sprang so hard the tentacles extended
out in front of it like arrows being shot. Cement and brick popped up,
this way and that, snapping like shrapnel.

It was quite the show, the way that machine leaped.

The Martians had never seen anything like it. They didn't know the
machines would do that, and they had built them.

---

got to give it to the humans, they are working that machine some
good, they are, the one assholed pieces of cosmic shit.

yes. (cough) damn. i'm getting a sore throat.

mind the controls.

i'm minding them.

mind them better.

are you trying to tell me how to (cough)...i'm not feeling so good.

now that you mention it, neither am i.

By this point, there wasn't much left of the Martian corpse in
Rikwalk's hand, having slammed and smashed it against the side of
the tower clock like he was dusting a rug. He threw the creature's
remains down at one of the machines attacking him. But it missed and
fell splattering into the street.

Primitive ape behavior had taken over. Rikwalk ripped off his
pants. He grabbed his dick and shook it at them. He dropped his dick
and shit in his hand and threw the shit. He hit the windshield of one
of the stalking towers, blurring the sight of the Martians inside.

The others closed in around the tower. They couldn't miss with
their death rays now. They lifted their heads, pointed their rays up.

Rikwalk waited for the big pop.

One moment, he thought, I am standing here, and the next
moment I'll be nothing more than a blazing hairball with a hand full
of shit (for he had filled up again).

He opened his eyes, determined to take it head on.

Then he saw bounding toward him another Martian machine. Behind it came five others. In the distance, lying in the street, he could see two others struggling to extricate themselves from one another.

The machine running toward him was the one containing his friends.

He raised the shit-filled hand, said, "Howdy, and so long."

The Martian machines had the clock surrounded now.

They aimed their rays.

And Big Ben struck the time.

That close, the whole earth shook.

Rikwalk certainly shook.

And he fell.

The rays blasted the air where he had been.

Rikwalk let go of the handful of shit. He wasn't that fond of it anyway.

He grabbed at the side of the clock tower, slipped (shit is greasy), grabbed again, and this time he caught a ridge, and hung there. Rikwalk dangled like a comma in a sentence.

"Help!" he said.

The Martians were surprised by the ape's sudden drop and his loud yell. They tried to refocus their attack. And would have too, but now, things had really changed.

Not only were our heroes coming—

But so was Steam.

Only he didn't know it yet.

———◆◆———

You see, Steam was pressed up against the other side of the clock tower all the while.

Way it worked was like this:

The Martians thought he was part of the tower. A kind of statue standing next to the entryway. Standing tall. A symbol that let loose a bit of smoke from its top from time to time.

They didn't know he had fire in his belly. They didn't know he could move.

Steam stood there, hands on his hips, in plain sight all through the night and through the morning, like a statue, being passed by the

Martian machines. The Martians had looked at him as if he were part of the clock tower.

Inside, where Beadle, John Feather and Passepartout waited, Beadle said, "Sometimes, I'm so smart I amaze my own goddamn self."

"You the man," John Feather said.

But that was then and this was now, and Steam, he moved.

Because, you see, inside of the metal man, Passepartout said, "That yell. No one sounds like that but Rikwalk. That's his strange voice. I'd know it anywhere."

"Then we have to help him," Beadle said. "No matter what the cost."

Beadle and John Feather put their hands on the controls, moved them. Steam stepped away from the clock, turned and walked around the edge of the tower, in the direction of the cry.

Simultaneously, all about and above them, the sky began ripping open in rips of red and blue, purple and yellow, and one rip of a very nice color that was somewhere between green and blue.

Twenty-two

A Ferocious Battle,
Strange Happenings, Herbert Wells

"It's happening," Beadle said, seeing the rips through the stained glass eyes of Steam. "Worlds are coming asunder."

"We must concentrate on the matter at hand," Passepartout said. "All else can wait, or happen without us."

"Oh, it will do that all right," Beadle said. "See there."

Passepartout looked.

A large boat came sailing out of one of the rips, hit the street, slid, crashed into a building across the way.

"That's just the beginning," Beadle said. "Just the way it started on our world. And look there."

One of the Martian machines, near the blue rip, was straining against something unseen. Then it seemed to stretch. And then—

—it was sucked up through a crack in the sky like liquid through a syphon hose.

Old cracks were closing, and new ones were opening.

"The rips still have a hard time staying open," Beadle said.

"If our experience is a common one," John Feather said, "that will change."

But there was no more time for discussion. They had rounded the clock tower. Now they were looking directly at Martian machines. The machines had congregated at the front of Big Ben. Their round heads and their thick windshields were lifted skyward, toward what dangled from above.

Rikwalk.

Steam looked past them at the machines racing toward them. One of them was manned by none other than their friends Twain, Verne and Ned the Seal. They were clearly visible through the hole where the glass had been.

The Martian machines near the clock tower were so intent on their hanging prey they had not even noticed Steam's arrival. Steam grabbed the nearest machine by one of its vining legs, jerked it off the ground, and gripping it with both metal hands, began to swing it.

Steam whirled it over his head, came around and struck another of the devices full smack-a-doodle. The Martian machines slammed together hard, exploded glass, green ichor, assholes and tentacles.

The remaining machines turned on Steam, who stood holding one metal tentacle. Rays were fired. One ray struck the metal behemoth in the neck, sliced through it like a hot knife through butter, came in like a burst of light through a bullet hole, hit Passepartout in the head.

His head went—

—POOF.

Nothing more.

A little explosion. A poof. Then there were black ashes settling to the floor. The remainder of his body collapsed, kicked, and quit.

"Goddamn," John Feather said.

Another ray struck one of the stained glass eyes. Glass shards sprayed. Glass hit both Beadle and John Feather. A large piece went through John Feather's cheek and lodged there, the tip of it poking through his gums, against his teeth.

Beadle snatched at the controls. Steam rushed forward, hunkered down. His fists flew.

And they made contact. The sound of metal on metal was deafening. Sparks flew from the blows. Martian machines went to pieces, were knocked about.

A ray was fired. Steam lost the metal tip of another one of his fingers.

—————⊷⊶—————

Verne's, Twain's, and Ned's machine was right on top of the melee now. But instead of joining in they wheeled their machine and sent rays flying back at their pursuers.

Rays jumped out of the Martians they were attacking. The sky was dotted with light. There were so many rays, and they came so fast, it was as if someone were tossing stiff confetti.

And then a strange thing happened.

The foremost pursuer fell.

Just fell over.

Toppled and hit the ground with a thud, went skidding along on the pavement, sparks leaping up like startled red and yellow frogs.

"What the hell?" Twain said.

But there was no time to wonder. In the background, the two machines that had entangled their legs were now disengaged. They were up and coming.

Everyone and everything weighed in.

It looked like a bar fight.

Steam was throwing machines this way and that. Verne, Twain, and Ned were too close to use their ray, feared they might hit Steam. But they swung one tentacle like a whip while they supported themselves on the other two.

They snapped it here. They snapped it there. Shattering windshields, popping exposed Martians. They scooped with it, jerking Martians out of broken windshields, slapping them on the ground, grabbing machine legs, tugging them out from under the machines, smashing them to the turf.

"They're not that quick-witted," Twain said. "They can build a machine, but they don't have imagination. They fight like sissies."

The other machines arrived.

The brawl went on.

The Martians didn't mind using their rays close in.

But this didn't work well for them. They quickly wiped out three of their own allies.

A few Martians escaped from broken windshields, or screwed open the plug trap doors, hustled down ladders, (Ned thought: Hey, where's our ladder? How come we don't have a ladder?) scuttled onto the ground, looking for hiding places.

They didn't find many.

Twain and Verne were pretty good shots with their ray. They cooked the Martians on the street bricks quicker than Ned could write:

FASTER, FASTER, KILL, KILL.

There was a pause now.

The calm after the storm.

Steam extended a hand.

The machine extended a tentacle.

They shook.

Then, without really talking about it, the Martian machine Twain and Verne operated clambered up on top of Steam, stretched two tentacles high, clung to Steam with the other, coiling it around his head like a constrictor crushing its prey.

The tentacles grabbed hold of Rikwalk, who had climbed down even closer, and lifted him on top of Steam. Rikwalk climbed down the metal man quickly, stood happily on the ground.

No sooner was this done than Steam made a noise and froze up like a rust-encrusted bolt.

A ladder was dropped out of Steam's ass. Beadle and John Feather climbed down, John pulling the glass from his cheek as soon as he descended.

Twain and Verne caused the Martian machine to coil its legs beneath its body, bringing it down to the ground. They unscrewed the plug and came out, Ned dragging the cruiser after him.

"Out of fuel," Beadle said. "We'll have to leave Steam. We were operating damn near off residue. We're lucky we lasted as long as we did."

"I think it's time we leave our machine as well," Twain said. "We're a little conspicuous. And it's taken a lot of damage."

"We are close to Herbert's home," Verne said. "We must try to find him. Where is Passepartout?"

"He is gone," Beadle said. "A ray struck him. He never knew what hit him."

"My God," Verne said. "Passepartout. My butler. My friend."

"I feel for you, sir," Beadle said, "but now is not the time to grieve. We must move on."

———⊰·⊱———

The cruiser carried them all except Rikwalk. It was a tight fit in the device and it moved more slowly than usual, bearing the excess weight. It barely skimmed above the ground. But it carried them.

Rikwalk ran beside them, using his foreknuckles to propel him.

As they went, they were surprised to see Martian machines lying about. Both the stalking machines and the triangular flying craft; several of them had crashed, tearing apart, spraying the premises with residue of Martians.

"What happened to them?" Twain said.

"Perhaps there are freedom fighters," Beadle said. "People working from the shadows, like us."

"It's not that shadowy right now," Twain said.

They wound down amongst broken, smoking stones, along damaged walls and trampled gardens, and finally came to a row of houses. The homes had all suffered damage, but appeared to be in reasonable condition.

Verne pointed at the largest of the row. "That is Herbert's home. We'll check."

"Careful he doesn't shoot you for a looter," Twain said.

—=◆=—

Rikwalk crouched in the courtyard, a sharp eye out for machines, as the others tried the door.

It came open.

They went inside.

Verne slumped. Though the house looked fine from the outside, inside the back wall had been knocked down, and the interior had been gutted by fire. The floor was littered with charred remains.

"Damn," Verne said. "Our last hope. Another friend gone. God. Is life worth living anymore?"

"It hasn't been for me for a long time," Twain said. "Until now. Until we banded together. With a cause. We have a reason, Jules. I almost forgot it's better to go down fighting than to not fight at all."

"Right now, I am all out of fight," Verne said.

Rikwalk yelled out from the courtyard.

Twenty-three/Epilogue

From the Journal of Ned the Seal:
The End of It All, Almost

When we went outside, me on the cruiser, the others on foot, to respond to Rikwalk's cries, we were surprised to see that above the courtyard a triangular machine was wobbling in the air.

"We have to flee," Verne said.

"No," Rikwalk said. "Watch. It's lost control."

The machine vibrated violently, sailed past us, dipped into a house across the way, exploded in a ball of fire. The heat from the explosion made my whiskers curl.

"Something is happening to them," Verne said.

"No shit," Twain said.

"Microbes."

We wheeled at the sound of the voice.

Standing at the back of the courtyard was a stocky mustached man.

"Herbert," Mr. Verne said.

"I am surprised, but glad to see you, my friend," the man said. "Your head is bandaged."

Mr. Verne said, "It's nothing, Herbert." Then to us: "This is H. G. Wells, gentlemen."

I wrote:

I READ *THE TIME MACHINE*.

"Holy shit," Mr. Wells said. "A seal that can write."

"A long story," Mr. Verne said.

IT WAS A GOOD BOOK.

"Alas, a bit of reporting on my part, Mr. Seal, and part of a greater concern, that story is. But that is not a story for this moment."

We paused at this mysterious reply, but Mr. Wells offered no more explanation.

"We saw the house," Mr. Verne said. "We thought you were dead."

"Come. We are still not safe. This ape, is he trained?"

"Oh my, yes," Rikwalk said. "But I don't do tricks."

"My God," Mr. Wells said. "He talks. A seal that writes, and an ape that talks. And a big ape he is."

"It's a convoluted story," Mr. Verne said. "These are our friends Mr. Beadle, and John Feather, Ned the Seal, and Rikwalk, from an alternate Mars. This is Samuel Clemens, better know as Mark Twain."

"Amazing," Mr. Wells said. "We will share our stories. But not here. Come, the back way."

We went through the courtyard gate, around to the back of the house where it had been knocked down.

Mr. Wells said, "I see that the fuel cell worked in Passepartout's design for the cruiser...Where is Passepartout?"

Mr. Verne hung his head. Mr. Twain said, "Rubbed out."

"I am sorry. Your family, Jules?"

I thought: The family jewels? Now is that a proper question?

"My wife and child left me long ago."

Oh. Never mind, I understood now.

"They felt I was too preoccupied with stories and reporting the events around me. They ran off with Phileas Fogg."

"I never liked him," Mr. Wells said. "Too, I don't know...Too too. Come. Look at this."

—◆—

Mr. Wells bent down and pulled back a large piece of wood, and underneath it were stairs.

"They didn't destroy the basement. I've been hiding down there. I was down here when the house was attacked. Come. I have lights controlled by the same type of fuel cell that runs the cruiser. It's quite comfortable, actually."

"You clever rascal," Mr. Verne said.

"Of course."

We went downstairs, me by cruiser, Rikwalk narrowing his shoulders. Fortunately, it was a wide opening, and he was able to make it, though the stairs creaked in a frightening manner under his weight.

Mr. Wells pushed the board back over the hole, and we remained in the dark until Mr. Wells managed his way downstairs and hit a switch.

The room lit up.

Above us and along the walls were long bars that generated light.

The room was huge. Packed with rows and rows of books. They rose all the way to the ceiling and there was a rolling ladder that went around the room to give access to them. There was also a lot of fine, comfortable looking furniture. Through a doorway I could see a lab, and beyond that, another open doorway and another room.

"Please, sit," Mr. Wells said. "Rest."

There was plenty of space. I climbed down from the cruiser and stretched out on a lounge. I lay there as if I had been harpooned. The events of the last few days were catching up with me. Mr. Twain and Mr. Verne sat and sighed, feeling the years creep up on them. Until that moment, they really hadn't had time to be old, and I hadn't actually noticed how elderly they seemed. Mr. Verne's beard, which I presume had been dyed black, now showed silver at the roots near his face, and it was the same for his hair. Mr. Twain had grown a bit of a beard, and it matched the white hair on his head. The lines on his face were as deep as ditches.

Beadle and John Feather found soft chairs. They sat back and stretched out their feet. Rikwalk curled on the floor, rested his head on his arm.

"I feel like an old dog crawled up my ass and died," Mr. Twain said.

"That is unique," Mr. Wells said.

"If I was any more tuckered out, I'd have to be buried," Mr. Twain said.

"We will try to hold off on that," Mr. Wells said.

"This is incredible," Mr. Beadle said. "All that destruction above, and here you are, safe and sound, thank goodness."

"It is quite the haven," Mr. Wells said. "But I have had my adventures on the outside as well. I was out scrounging for more food today. I have a large supply set in. I even have a refrigeration machine that is run by the fuel cell I discovered that operates the cruiser. It is amazing stuff. It is not an invention, I might add, but a discovery. Anyway,

I was out scrounging, and I saw more and more of the machines crashing. Martians dying. I took one of the machines apart one night, and I found many things of interest inside. I have them in the laboratory. They are very advanced technologically. But that aside, they are not as smart as one might suspect."

"You said something about microbes," Mr. Verne said.

"Exactly," Mr. Wells said. "Fate has stepped in to weigh on our side. The Martians do not have our immunity to such simple things as a summer cold. All manner of diseases that we deal with every day are little devils to them. They are over laden with our microbes, and now they are dying. It is just a matter of time, and it is all over."

"My God," Verne said. "That is why they are starting to collapse, why there were so many dead Martians lying about."

"Correct," Mr. Wells said. "It started a day or so ago, and I've been waiting them out. Though, foolishly, I went about trying to secure even more food today. It was an unnecessary chance, and, alas, I had no real luck. Within a week, I predict, the invaders will be no more."

"Then all we do is wait," Mr. Twain said.

"Of course," Mr. Beadle said, "happy as that all is, we have the problem of the rips."

Mr. Wells nodded. "Yes. The rips. The tears in time."

"You know about all this?" Mr. Verne said. "How did you know what they were? Beadle and John Feather told us. They are from another time. As is Rikwalk. But how did you know?"

"Because of the Time Traveler. The star of my book *The Time Machine*. I reported his adventures as he told them to me. He was my friend once upon a time. I fear he is the cause."

"He is," Beadle said, and told Mr. Wells the story he had told us.

"It appears it is too late to do anything," John Feather said, "if there is anything that can be done."

"Possibly," Mr. Wells said. "But it would involve traveling in time. I feel almost responsible. I made a hero out of him, and a hero he was not."

"You could not have known," Mr. Verne said.

"We have the Time Traveler's diary in the machine we abandoned," John Feather said. "It might help."

"Yes," Mr. Wells said, "it might. The last time I saw the Time

Traveler he had grown quite mad. He left, and I never saw him again. But now, Mr. Beadle, I understand what has happened to him."

"Yeah," John Feather said, "we fucked him over good. But he had it coming."

"No doubt," Mr. Wells said. "But once he was my friend. And whole. A good man. I must give him that."

"You don't get as bad as he was without some character flaw somewhere," Beadle said. "And I doubt it was just bad bathroom habits. Early on, he was askew. It just took stress to show his true character."

"Perhaps, but what matters is this," Mr. Wells said. "If we can travel the paths he made in time, reversing the energy on the machine, we can pull the corridors back together as we travel through. Tighten up the universe. Stop this collapse. I think."

"If that is true," Mr. Beadle said, "If it can be done, we would need a time machine to make it work. And we would have to know all the paths the Time Traveler took."

"Right you are," Mr. Wells said. "Remember, he was my friend. I know a lot about him. A lot I did not report in the book. As for where he went, and how to follow, a companion machine would naturally be pulled into those corridors. The idea is to follow the paths, then reverse them. Close the time tunnels off."

"He traveled so much," Mr. Beadle said.

"Then," Mr. Wells said, "so will we. But not until this Martian menace is certainly defeated by our heroic microbes."

"And how will we travel through time?" John Feather said.

"In this room, I have the plans my friend used for his machine, and I have applied them to the very structure of this room. There are still a few things to be done. Areas to be sealed. But in the very comfort of this room, these rooms, in fact, we, sirs, can travel through time."

I wrote:

THAT IS SOME REALLY NEAT SHIT.

"Yes, Ned," Mr. Wells said. "It is."

<hr/>

A week later, living off the supplies Mr. Wells had put aside, we ventured out one day near evening. London was in flames, but there were people trying to put out some of the fires. A fire engine drawn by four huge, tired horses clunked by, wearing men hanging on the sides of it. It was somehow reassuring to see vestiges of civilization returning. Soon, I presumed fish markets would be back in business, and fish could be purchased at most any time of day. The idea of that intrigued me. Any time of day without swimming about for them. A very merry idea, indeed.

The wrecked Martian machines were everywhere.

So were a lot of people.

They had come out to finish off the few Martian survivors, beating them with bats and clubs. And they looted anything of interest they could find in the machines.

In a huge pile near Big Ben, near where Steam still stood, they had piled Martian bodies and were burning them.

We joined in, dragging the invaders to the pile.

Well, I actually watched. I wasn't suited for moving too swiftly over the streets on my belly. I rode about in my cruiser.

I wrote a lot of notes about what people should be doing.

No one gave me any mind.

Maybe it was becoming too dark to read my signs.

No one asked about me or about Rikwalk, who was carrying the stinking Martians by the armload to the pyre. They had other concerns and had become accustomed to strange things coming through the time and space rips. And it was obvious to them that Rikwalk and myself were helping dispose of the Martians.

I did see one dead dinosaur lying nearby. A long very big thing with tree trunk legs that looked something like the *Brontosaurus* I had seen in books, but his head was different. And he was brightly colored, like a bird. He had started to decay. It was my guess the creature had come through a rip and gotten into a battle with a Martian machine, and had lost to a death ray. Part of his chest was gone. The tip of his nose, about the size of Rikwalk's head, was rolled up against a wall and was covered in happy flies.

The body of Passepartout, or what remained of it, was pulled out of Steam, stinking and dissolving, and put on the pyre along with the invaders. It was all that could be done under the circumstances. The diary of the Time Traveler was rescued and kept by Mr. Beadle.

According to Mr. Beadle, it was lucky it had not been destroyed, as much of the machine's interior had been sabotaged and stripped of anything worthy by looters. Even Passepartout had been stripped of his shoes, jacket, and pants.

Mr. Verne said a prayer for Passepartout, and we watched his remains climb to the sky in smoke.

And that was that.

—◦•◦—

When the day was done, we made our way back to Mr. Wells' home, avoiding others lest they might want to follow us and take our food. People had worked together on this day, but there was an air of anarchy, and we did not want to be recipients of it.

It wasn't really much trouble, our going our own way without interference. We had Rikwalk with us. No one wanted to mess with him. And Mr. Verne had returned Mr. Beadle's rifle, which Mr. Beadle carried with an air of authority.

Still, we came to the street where Mr. Wells lived, and snuck into his basement cautiously. Just as I was about to drop downstairs on my cruiser, I looked up and saw a dragon fly across the face of the partial moon.

Not a good sign.

—◦•◦—

A Week Later—Ned's Journal Continued

And now I sit me down to write on the night we leave. Mr. Wells says we can move through time, and we can move through space, so we will actually change locations, not just travel through time.

That being, coming back could, I presume, result in complications.

Shit. I don't know. I am a Fez-wearing seal. Not some goddamn mathematician or scientist. I can barely boil water.

The room has been sealed and a special door has been fastened above the stairway where before there was only a large gap and a board to cover it.

The door is huge so that Rikwalk can come and go.

Out there, the world is coming apart.

We have water and food in here. Enough to last for some time. Even some canned fish, which is a good thing.

When the last bit of work is done on the machine—and this is being supervised by Mr. Verne and Mr. Wells, and the actual work is being accomplished by Mr. Beadle and John Feather—we will set asail on the seas of time.

If fate is with us, we will fix that which needs fixing.

If fate is not with us.

Then we will die trying.

Not on purpose, mind you. I mean, I'm going to try and live. Even if the world is full of harpooners and dinosaurs and pigs that fly and venomous snakes the size of Big Ben and a dragon that can fly across the face of the moon.

But you get the idea. This is heroic dime novel stuff.

And maybe you don't get the idea.

Maybe no one will read this.

That bothers me. I have used my best penmanship.

Of course, if the journal is in the machine with me, how will anyone read it?

Maybe later it will be read.

If we survive.

Even if we don't survive.

Maybe a flying pig will read it over our dead bodies. It could happen. Provided the pig can read, of course.

I really must rest.

I have been awake for way too many hours.

Ah, Mr. Verne is calling to me. They need me for some last minute repairs. (I don't know what I can do, but I'm glad to do it.)

And then, after we eat, canned fish, I hope, we're off.

—◆—

I'M BACK

—◆—

Damn thing wouldn't start up.

Isn't that typical. Someone crossed a wire or something.

But, hey, we haven't given up. A short break. A nap. And we'll try again.

And if there was someone out there who could wish us luck, someone who could read what I write as I write, I would want them to do that right now.

Wish us luck, I mean.

Luck is always good.

It would be nice if the machine worked, of course. That would be pretty handy, actually.

I have faith it will. And when it does, it will plunge us backward and forward through time, plugging holes like the little Dutch boy putting his finger in the dike. (I read that story in Doctor Momo's library long ago, and I am very proud of my reference to it. I think it is very appropriate, don't you?)

Ah, they call again. The nap is out. They are certain they have it, now.

Someone dropped a fish down there in the wall wiring, they say. They're not naming names, but they have an idea. The fish shorted out the wires. But now all is good. I hope they didn't toss the fish away.

We are going to gather in the main room, sit on the couch, the control box in Mr. Wells' lap. He will flip a switch, twist a dial, and off we will go, a chuggy-whuggy through time.

By God, it will be a great adventure.